PENGUIN

THE ADVENTURES

CARLO COLLODI (1826–1890) was the pen name of Carlo Lorenzini, an Italian author, journalist, translator, critic, and satirist, born in Florence. A passionate supporter of the ideals of the Risorgimento, the movement that united Italy and freed it from foreign domination, he fought in both of Italy's Wars of Independence. He also cofounded the patriotic satirical daily *Il Lampione*. In 1875, perhaps disillusioned with the politics of post-Unification Italy, he turned to writing children's stories. But he did not abandon satire. His masterpiece, *Le avventure di Pinocchio: Storia di un burattino,* was originally published in installments that began to appear in 1881 in a newspaper for children, *Giornale per i bambini*, and published in book form in 1883. It is laced with wry comments on Italian society, some as relevant today as they were in the late nineteenth century.

JOHN HOOPER is Italy and Vatican correspondent of *The Economist* and the author of the bestseller *The Italians*. He has reported from Italy for more than twenty years. Hooper is a lecturer at the Florence campus of Stanford University and an Honorary Fellow of St Catharine's College, University of Cambridge.

ANNA KRACZYNA is a native of Florence, the daughter of American artists who moved to Italy. She has taught at the Florence campuses of Stanford University and Sarah Lawrence College, and divides her time among translating, interpreting, and lecturing at American universities in her native city on the language, literature, and society of Italy.

CARLO COLLODI

The Adventures of Pinocchio

STORY OF A PUPPET

Translated, with an Introduction and Notes, by
JOHN HOOPER *and* ANNA KRACZYNA

PENGUIN BOOKS

PENGUIN BOOKS

An imprint of Penguin Random House LLC
penguinrandomhouse.com

Originally published in Italian as *Le avventure di Pinocchio: storia di un burattino*
by Felice Paggi Libraio–Editore, 1883.

This book was translated thanks to a grant awarded by the Italian Ministry of
Foreign Affairs and International Cooperation.

LIBRARY OF CONGRESS CATALOGING-IN-PUBLICATION DATA
Names: Collodi, Carlo, 1826–1890, author. | Hooper, John, 1950– translator. |
Kraczyna, Anna, translator.
Title: The adventures of Pinocchio : story of a puppet / Carlo Collodi ;
translated with an introduction and notes by John Hooper and Anna Kraczyna.
Other titles: Avventure di Pinocchio. English
Description: New York : Penguin Books, 2021. | Includes bibliographical references.
Identifiers: LCCN 2021017046 (print) | LCCN 2021017047 (ebook) |
ISBN 9780143136095 (paperback) | ISBN 9780525507666 (ebook)
Subjects: CYAC: Fairy tales. | Puppets—Fiction.
Classification: LCC PZ8.C7 Ad 2021 (print) | LCC PZ8.C7 (ebook) | DDC [Fic]—dc23
LC record available at https://lccn.loc.gov/2021017046
LC ebook record available at https://lccn.loc.gov/2021017047

Printed in the United States of America
4th Printing

Set in Sabon LT Pro

Contents

Introduction

This is a book with a mission: to rescue Pinocchio. More precisely, the intention of this annotated translation is to save Carlo Collodi's *The Adventures of Pinocchio*, the book that first brought the puppet to life, from being imprisoned in a category labeled "Children's Stories." The *Adventures* was, of course, intended for children. But not only for children. Its author was a writer of immense culture and great sophistication, and he told his story with a brilliant use of language. But he also wove into his narrative multiple strands of meaning, and we have sought to tease them out with comprehensive endnotes that highlight many of the subtleties waiting to be discovered in a text that is far more complex than generally realized.

The gap between the way Collodi's book is perceived in the land of its origin and the view taken of it by speakers of English is vast. In Italy, critics regard it as a masterpiece: one of the greatest works in the literary canon; a book that has played a significant role in the development of the Italian language; one rich in subtle allusions and artful contrivances, comparable to *Alice's Adventures in Wonderland* or *Gulliver's Travels*. Italian scholars have written extensively on the layers of cultural, social, political, and even religious significance to be found in it.

Many English speakers, by contrast, are more likely to have had their perceptions of the story colored by Walt Disney's 1940 cartoon movie version, *Pinocchio*. Seldom has a work of literature been so overshadowed by its celluloid adaptation.

The *Adventures* was not unknown outside Italy before Disney's animators got to work on it. It was published in an English translation in 1891, just eight years after it appeared in

Italian, and soon became popular in the English-speaking world and beyond. But it was Disney's motion picture that transformed Collodi's puppet into a universally recognizable character. The *Adventures* has since gone on to be one of the world's two most translated works of fiction[1]; it has been re-incarnated in TV series, plays, video games, and other movies; the puppet's name has been given to an asteroid and used to denote a philosophical conundrum—all largely because of the global fame conferred on him by Hollywood.

One reason for this is that Disney's movie was a landmark in the history of animation. It introduced an extraordinary degree of realism with effects so far ahead of their time that, even today, they do not look particularly outdated. But Disney and his animators did more than just tweak Collodi's original tale. They distorted the personality of the central character, replaced the message at the heart of the fable, and changed the setting.

Disney's *Pinocchio* is about a cute little boy who tells the odd fib. Collodi's puppet, by contrast, is a brat. The original Pinocchio has a good—even, at times, noble—heart. And toward the end of the *Adventures* he starts to mature. But until then, he is lazy, mischievous, irresponsible, profoundly egotistical, and easily led astray: a late nineteenth-century prototype for the likes of Bart Simpson.

Collodi's Pinocchio is also intermittently mendacious. And on a couple of occasions the author punishes him for his lies by making his nose grow. Disney, with a sharp eye for a visually arresting novelty, homed in on the puppet's extending nose, making it central to his movie in a way that it is not in the book. The result was to forge a link between Pinocchio and lying that has since become indissoluble. The emoji for a lie is a face with an absurdly long nose, and when *The Washington Post*'s fact-checkers scrutinize politicians' assertions, they rate them on a scale from no Pinocchios to four. Yet it is hard to read Collodi's original story as a cautionary tale about the evils and consequences of lying.

The fable began as a serial, *Storia di un burattino* (*Story of a Puppet*). The first installment was published in the launch issue of the *Giornale per i bambini*, or *Newspaper for Children*, on

July 7, 1881. Both the periodical and the series enjoyed instant popularity. Collodi continued to chronicle Pinocchio's misadventures until he brought them to a shockingly grisly end in October, when the puppet was left hanging from a tree, apparently dead. By then, Pinocchio's nose *had* grown. Twice. But—as we point out in the endnotes—not when he lied. When he did lie, his nose did not extend by even a millimeter. So, had the story ended when its author intended, the link would never have been made.

Such, however, was the clamor from readers for the tale to be continued that its author resumed *Storia di un burattino* in the same newspaper four months later and sustained it through an additional nineteen installments before definitively ending his story in January 1883, when the entire tale was repackaged as a book, *Le avventure di Pinocchio: Storia di un burattino* (*The Adventures of Pinocchio: Story of a Puppet*). Even in the second run of installments, however, the puppet's nose grows on only two occasions in response to his lying. What is more, the puppet tells at least three, and arguably four, other lies in the second part of the story without anything untoward happening to his nose. Mendacity was in no way central to Collodi's original work.

Other messages lay at the heart of the tale. As Daniela Marcheschi notes in her monumental annotated edition of a selection of Collodi's works,[2] Collodi was a great believer in the "university of life"—children learning from their mistakes and building up a stock of experience with which to cope with the perils and opportunities of life. But at a time when schooling was only just starting to become compulsory in Italy, he was also an advocate of the need for formal education. Pinocchio's reluctance to go to school is the driving force behind the plot of the *Adventures*. It is what leads him from one disaster to the next. Ultimately, it results in his being turned into a donkey. In Italian, the words for "donkey" (*asino, somaro,* and *ciuco*) all have several meanings in addition to the literal one: they are applied to those who do not do well in school (and not necessarily because they are stupid, but because they fail to apply themselves) and to those who are worked to the point of exhaustion, or even death. Collodi's message to children, at a time when the life of an unskilled laborer was one of unremitting hardship, was that if they insisted on being "donkeys" at school, they risked living the life, and maybe dying the death, of a donkey in adult life.

A second, deeper theme is the growth to maturity via the acquiring of a sense of responsibility. It is only after Pinocchio starts to care for his "parents," Geppetto the carpenter and the Blue-haired Fairy, that he earns the right to be a human being. The twin morals of the story, it can be argued, are that education is vital and, more important, that a sense of duty to others is at the core of our common humanity. Some of that, though more of the latter than the former, found its way into Disney's film.

The most drastic change that Hollywood made was to thoroughly de-Italianize the story. Some of the characters have names ending in *o*. But that is about as Italian as it gets. *Pinocchio* the movie is set in some ill-defined, mountainous European land. Geppetto is transformed from a dirt-poor Tuscan carpenter into a maker of cuckoo clocks and other sophisticated timepieces. Pinocchio is given an Alpine hat with a feather stuck in the ribbon around the brim. And he and his creator are shown living together happily in a town of half-timbered houses with steeply pitched roofs.

But then the film was crafted as the shadow of Italian Fascism, allied to German Nazism, was creeping across Europe. It was released in the same year that Italy's dictator, Benito Mussolini, declared war on Britain and France, America's oldest allies in Europe. The following year, 1941, Italy declared war on the United States itself. It was not a moment to be setting a cartoon movie, however entrancing, in Italy. Yet Italy, and specifically Carlo Collodi's native Tuscany, is at the very core of a story written by a man who was passionate about his homeland and the destiny of his compatriots.

Carlo Collodi is a pseudonym. The real name of the author of the *Adventures* was Carlo Lorenzini. He was born in Florence in 1826. His father was the cook in an aristocratic household, that of the Marquis Ginori Lisci. Lorenzini's mother trained as an elementary school teacher, but found it more remunerative to work as the Marchioness's seamstress. While his parents were in straitened circumstances, the young Lorenzini spent long periods of his childhood with his mother's relatives, in the town of Collodi, forty miles northwest of Florence. It is indicative of the rudimentary medical care available to families like his in nineteenth-century Italy that, of Lorenzini's nine siblings, only three should have reached adulthood: five died before the age of seven, a sixth when she was sixteen.

While still at school, Lorenzini took a job in Florence at the Piatti bookshop, which was also a publishing house and a meeting place for the city's intellectuals, many passionately committed to the causes of liberalism, democracy, and Italian Unification. In 1848, as revolution swept through Europe, Lorenzini volunteered to fight the Austrians then ruling much of northern Italy, in what came to be known as the First War of Independence. After the Italians were defeated, he returned to Florence, where he helped found *Il Lampione*, a satirical review with a democratic agenda that became one of the foremost periodicals of its time. He was to continue writing political satire for the rest of his life. An admirer of Giuseppe Mazzini, the leading ideologue of the Risorgimento (Reawakening) that led to Unification, Lorenzini had initially been a republican. But in common with many of his fellow patriots, he gradually came to accept that the only way Italy would be united was as a monarchy under the auspices of King Vittorio Emanuele II, the ruler of Sardinia and Piedmont. It was in that spirit that in 1859 Lorenzini enrolled in the king's army to fight in the Second War of Independence, also against the Austrians, but this time with the support of the French. This conflict forced the Austrians to withdraw from their Italian territories and cleared the way for Unification.

Twice, then, Lorenzini risked his life to help found the independent and united Italy that was proclaimed in 1861.[3] As the new state's politics became increasingly sleazy and its politicians progressively less concerned with the poverty of the majority of its citizens, Lorenzini felt a profound sense of betrayal, which may well explain why he embraced the then-novel genre of children's fiction: that, despairing of his contemporaries, he decided the best contribution he could make was to invest his talents in improving the ethical caliber of future generations.

While some of his messages can seem conservative today, Collodi was no reactionary by the standards of his time. He was a liberal, even a radical, and his most celebrated story reflects a deep concern for the social inequality that he saw in Italy. The *Adventures* is a fairy tale without princes or princesses, knights or damsels. Its setting is one that the author knew only too well: the harsh world of the rural poor—much the same as that of Ermanno Olmi's 1978 art house classic, *The Tree of Wooden Clogs*. Though Olmi's movie unfolds in Lombardy rather than Tuscany, his characters, like those in the *Adventures*, are the little people of late nineteenth-century Italy. Collodi uses his fable to hint at the injustices to which they are subject and for which they have no redress. And again and again, he returns to the themes of hunger and misery. It is there right at the beginning, in the description of Geppetto's wretched living conditions, and hangs over the rest of the book like a dark cloud.

As one essayist has written, the *Adventures* presents "a picture of an Italy—of a country of hovels and fishing villages—that struggles every day to survive. . . . Its protagonists are healthy and generous in spirit, but vexed by the powerful and cheated by their fraudulent advisers."[4] In this respect, Collodi's work has every claim to a place in the corpus of nineteenth-century novels of social denunciation. It may contain more humor than many books written for children (and certainly more than most written in the nineteenth century), but it is also infused with a pervasive melancholy that arises from its author's despondency over the state of the nation he had helped to form.

Like other great works of fiction, the *Adventures* operates on several levels. It is a bildungsroman, an extended metaphor of how a child grows to maturity, and—not least—a satire. Though for much of his life Collodi earned his living as a public employee, he pursued a literary career of vast scope. Long before he began producing books for children, he had written about music, theater, art, and literature. He edited periodicals, authored plays, and translated books (from French). But throughout his life he remained a polemical journalist, and in many respects his chronicle of Pinocchio's exploits is an extension of his criticism of the way in which post-Unification Italy was being governed. It also takes an often wry look at aspects of Italian society that are as characteristic today as they were in the 1880s.

That Collodi—or at least his publisher—saw the *Adventures* in that light is evident from the way the book was presented to the public on its first appearance. An advertisement in the *Corriere del Mattino* of February 14, 1883, declared that readers would find in it "the quintessence of Italian good sense grafted onto the most uncompromising humor." Collodi and his publishers were clearly being ironic about the Italian good sense, since most of what is described in the novel does not reflect good sense at all. The uncompromising humor, on the other hand, is everywhere. As an example of Collodi's satire, take the passage in which Pinocchio has been seized by a farmer and put to work as a watchdog in place of one that has just died. He is chained up in a little shed in the farmyard when along comes a weasel with a dodgy proposition:

"We'll come over to visit the chicken coop once a week, as we have done in the past, and we'll take away eight hens. We'll eat seven of the hens and give you one, on condition—obviously— that you pretend you're asleep and that it never even occurs to you to bark and wake up the farmer."

What the weasel is offering is what today would be known as a 12.5 percent kickback or—to use the Italian term—*tangente*. Whether the paying of *tangenti* is any less prevalent today than it was in Collodi's day is unknowable. But it certainly remains a part of Italian business and political life, to the extent that some Italians do not even regard it as corruption. Individuals negotiating to place a contract on behalf of a company will often expect to receive a small percentage of its value (a good deal less than 12.5 percent) from the prospective supplier; similarly, politicians and officials will sometimes demand a cut in return for the award of public contracts (though, in the case of politicians, the *tangente* is meant to be for their party's coffers rather than for personal gain).

In the Cold War years, *tangenti* became so prevalent that, as shown by a scandal that erupted in the early 1990s and came to be known as Tangentopoli, Italy's entire postwar political order had come to rely on them. The main parties were funding their extensive activities, their lavish electoral campaigns, and, in some cases, the extravagant lifestyles of their senior officials with commissions levied on public contracts for everything from the building of city subways to the supply of toilet paper to nursing homes for the elderly.

The prosecutors who lit the fuse on Tangentopoli were, in a sense, the spiritual descendants of Pinocchio, who blows the whistle on his putative business partners and is rewarded for his honesty. The weasels end up stewed in a sweet and sour sauce, which is a distinctly worse fate than awaited the thousands of officials, intermediaries, financiers, industrialists, and elected representatives caught up in Tangentopoli. Some were acquitted. Others plea-bargained. But many benefited from the torpidity of the Italian judicial system and had their cases dismissed after they were timed out by a statute of limitations. Only a handful ever served prison sentences.

For most Italians, the outcome of Tangentopoli was yet another reason for cynicism about the workings of their judicial system—a cynicism that stretches back centuries and finds one of its most patent, yet humorous, expressions in the *Adventures*. When Pinocchio goes to court, he finds that the judge hearing his case is an ape. After listening sympathetically to Pinocchio's complaint that he has been tricked and robbed, the judge orders Pinocchio to be thrown in jail for being ingenuous.

So here is a tale—written for children, remember—in which one of the morals is "Don't expect justice if you turn to the courts," and another is "If you're gullible, you're going to be made to pay for it." The same bleak view underlies two of the occasions on which the police, in the shape of the Carabinieri, appear in the story. In both instances, they arrest the wrong "person": first, Geppetto, and later, Pinocchio.

But going back for a moment to Collodi's description of the judge, we find another of the author's sly digs at his compatriots. The judge was

a big, old ape, respected because of his honorable age, his white beard and *particularly* [our italics] his gold-rimmed glasses, which had no lenses and which he was forced to wear at all times because of an eye inflammation that had been tormenting him for years.

On the surface, this is just nonsensical, if mildly amusing. But seen from an Italian standpoint, it takes on a wealth of meaning. The judge is respected, above all, because he can afford expensive spectacles. And he makes sure that everyone is aware of his prosperity by wearing them at all times, even though he does not need them and has had to invent an absurd excuse for doing so. Collodi is taking aim, as he does on several occasions in the *Adventures*, at his compatriots' obsession with that quintessentially Italian concept of *bella figura*: giving the best possible impression to others. The judge wears costly but unnecessary glasses for the same reason many Italians who can barely afford essentials drive expensive cars and wear designer clothes. Collodi is mocking not only the judge but also the values of the people the judge seeks to impress. By attributing greater weight to the judge's affluence than to his experience, let alone his learning or judgment, which are not even mentioned, his fellow citizens—Collodi seems to say—get the justice they deserve.

A similarly irreverent view infuses the passage of the book in which its author turns his gaze on the medical profession. The three doctors called to Pinocchio's bedside after he narrowly escapes death for the first time are made out to be utter incompetents. But before the doctors deliver their ludicrous opinions on the puppet's health, Collodi makes a subtler point, though whether he does so intentionally is debatable. After having Pinocchio brought to her house, the Fairy "summoned the most famous doctors in the neighborhood." Not the best, but the most *famous*—an intimation of the consideration that Italians have for other people's opinions and that is to be found at the heart of *bella figura*. Collodi's characters repeatedly demonstrate by their words or actions their concern for the way in which they appear to the rest of the world.

Just as untranslatable as *bella figura* is another quintessentially Italian concept: *furbizia*. If you look in an Italian-English dictionary, the definitions you find are negative: cunning, sly, deceitful. These cover the meaning to some extent. But in Italian, *furbizia* is not always completely negative. There is a world of difference, for example, between *fare il furbo*, which means taking an unfair advantage, such as cutting a line, and *essere furbo*, which means knowing how to get your way in life, and which almost always attracts at least a tad of admiration. Where precisely *furbizia* should be located on the line that separates good from evil depends very much on circumstance and individual morality. But few Italians would quibble with the view that the *furbizia* of Pinocchio's two false friends, the Fox and the Cat, is of the worst kind: when thwarted in their efforts to shake him down, they are quite prepared to murder him. Before they reach that extreme, however, the Fox especially shows himself to be a master of delinquent *furbizia*: quick-witted, inventive, and duplicitous.

The chronicle of Pinocchio's exploits nevertheless also highlights a number of the Italians' fine qualities. At the core of the story is the importance of family ties. Pinocchio's supreme challenge, the test he must pass before he can become human, is to care for his "parents" in an age before retirement pensions and public health services. Like so many millions of Italians before and after, he does so uncomplainingly and in arduous circumstances.

This is all of a piece with a capacity for putting up with life's vicissitudes that is expressed in that most Italian of exclamations, *"Pazienza!"* It occurs no fewer than fifteen times in the *Adventures*. We have in most cases rendered it into English as "Oh well!" But it is as good an example as any of the notion that every translation is a betrayal. "Oh well" expresses a temporary acceptance of destiny's foibles: you win some; you lose some; tomorrow is another day. *"Pazienza!"* is far more profoundly fatalistic. It echoes centuries of unwilling yet unavoidable resignation. From the fall of the Roman Empire to the Unification of Italy, just a few years before Collodi wrote his masterpiece, many if not most of the inhabitants of the peninsula lived out their lives under foreign rulers over whom they could exercise little or no control. Those who inhabited the city-states of the north and part of the center were self-governing in medieval times, and that may help explain a greater sense of civic responsibility in those areas, but they were ultimately nevertheless subject to a German sovereign, the Holy Roman Emperor, who periodically interfered in the affairs of what is now Italy—and often with violent, even fatal, effects for the long-suffering Italians themselves.

This brings us to another point: since these foreign masters and mistresses had the power of life and death over their subjects, they needed to be humored. Small wonder, then, that the Italians developed a talent for flattery. One of the most striking examples of this is the extensive use of titles. They are at least as common today as when Collodi was alive. A lawyer (*Avvocato* or *Avvocatessa*), engineer (*Ingegnere*), accountant (*Ragioniere* or *Ragioniera*), lecturer (*Professore* or *Professoressa*) or medical doctor (*Dottore* or *Dottoressa*) will all expect to be addressed as such, even in relatively informal contexts. Anyone with a university degree also merits *Dottore* or *Dottoressa*, which causes a fair amount of confusion.

Faced with the terrifying puppeteer Fire-eater, Pinocchio knows exactly how to react. He immediately reaches for an appropriately hyperbolic title, and addresses him as "most illustrious sir." But it is when he needs a favor from Fire-eater—a vital one, to save the life of his friend Harlequin—that Pinocchio's instincts really come to the fore. He escalates the honorifics, enhancing the titles that he proffers to Fire-eater as he desperately tries to win him over.

> "Have pity, Mr. Fire-eater! . . ."
> "There are no misters here!" replied the puppeteer sternly.
> "Have pity, Mr. Knight! . . ."
> "There are no knights here!"
> "Have pity, Mr. Lord! . . ."
> "There are no lords here!"
> "Have pity, Your Excellency! . . ."

And, finally, it works:

> Hearing himself called Excellency, the puppeteer immediately pursed his lips tight, and having suddenly become more humane and approachable, he said to Pinocchio:
> "So then, what do you want from me?"

It has been argued that the very fact that Pinocchio is a puppet—that he is a creature without control of his destiny and susceptible to the manipulation of others—is part of the reason why Italians have taken him to their hearts. It is certainly striking that, as the novelist and screenwriter Raffaele La Capria wrote,[5] "perhaps the only charismatic character in Italian literature is a puppet."

What is unquestionably true is that Pinocchio is one of those rare fictional characters in whom an entire people seem to be able to make out their reflection. The only similar literary creations who spring to mind are Don Quixote and Sancho Panza, personifications of the twin souls of Spain: absurdly idealistic and earthily pragmatic. But what Carlo Collodi achieved was to bring together in a single character more than half a dozen of the contrasting traits that Italians, whether proudly or reluctantly, associate with themselves and their compatriots. For Gian Luigi Corinto, Pinocchio is "generous, good-hearted, open, combative, brattish, but a good son who risks his life to save his father, mendacious yet likeable—the most powerful ambassador for *italianità* [Italianness]."[6]

That same title might have been awarded to Pinocchio's creator, who turned what he initially dismissed as a *"bambinata"* (a bit of kid's stuff) into one of the best-known, and best-loved, stories in world literature. Carlo Collodi continued to write prolifically after the publication of the *Adventures*. Another of his stories told in installments, *Pipì lo scimmiottino color di rosa* (Pipì the Little Rose-Colored Monkey), enjoyed great success in Italy, and two books he had written earlier were published in even more editions than the *Adventures* during his lifetime. The man behind the pseudonym, Carlo Lorenzini, died suddenly in 1890. One of the journalists who covered his well-attended funeral wrote: "He was the teacher of us all: a teacher emulated by some, but excelled by none."[7]

JOHN HOOPER AND ANNA KRACZYNA

NOTES

1. The other is also a children's story, Antoine de Saint-Exupéry's *Le Petit Prince*.
2. Carlo Collodi, *Opere* (1995).
3. It was not until 1870, however, that the country became fully unified when Italian troops seized Rome from the pope, later making the city the capital of the new state.
4. Cosimo Ceccuti, *Carlo Collodi protagonista dell'Unità d'Italia* (2011).
5. Raffaele La Capria, *Letteratura e salti mortali* (1990).
6. Gian Luigi Corinto and Fabio Norcino, *Pinocchio Fiorentino: Mali antichi e antichi rimedi* (2020).
7. Eugenio Checchi in *Fanfulla della Domenica,* October 29, 1890.

A Note on the Translation

We have aimed to produce a translation that, while reading as easily as a modern novel, remains as faithful as possible to the character and flavor of Collodi's original text. Our translation is from Ornella Castellani Pollidori's definitive, critical edition prepared for the Fondazione Nazionale Carlo Collodi and published in 1983 to coincide with the hundredth anniversary of the publication of the novel.

The author of the *Adventures* was a writer of genius. One of his many virtues was to avoid not only clichés but also familiar, overused phrases, often devising metaphors and similes of his own. Faced with these inventions, the temptation is to reach for a roughly equivalent, instantly recognizable English phrase. But that would fail to honor the author's creativity. We therefore devised and applied a rule: if the obvious English phrase also existed in Italian, it was reasonable to suppose Collodi had made a deliberate choice to avoid it, and that we would be misrepresenting him if we instead were to use it.

Thus, in chapter 23, Pinocchio tells the Pigeon not that he is as light as a feather, which is as much of a cliché in Italian as it is in English, but as light as a leaf. And since that is perfectly comprehensible in English, we have gone with Collodi.

In the passage in which the unctuously sinister Little Man is taking the boys in a coach to Playland, Collodi describes them as being heaped, one on top of the other, *come tante acciughe nella salamoia*, "like so many anchovies in brine." The obvious translation is "like so many sardines in a can." But the same phrase exists in Italian, and Collodi did not use it. He turned instead to a much less common simile. Why? Very possibly because he was avoiding the more hackneyed phrase. But also perhaps because he wished to tap into another meaning of anchovy in Italian, which applies to someone who is lean and skinny. In the case of a crowd of little boys, that makes for a more vivid metaphor than one that depends on a plump sardine. So, as in other instances, we decided to remain faithful to the original, at the expense perhaps of jolting the reader with an unexpected comparison.

Collodi does sometimes employ common phrases and sayings, but in a way that is subtle and singular: he makes his characters act them out without their ever being spelled out on the page. This happens repeatedly in the *Adventures*. One example is in chapter 28, when the monstrous fisherman, reaching into his net, grabs hold of Pinocchio and says to himself that the puppet must be a deep-sea crab. In Italian, to catch a crab means to make a mistake.

The *Adventures* was written at a decisive moment in the evolution of Italian. The states that made up what is now Italy had been unified barely a decade earlier, and the inhabitants of the new country were being asked to adopt as their national language that of one of those states, the former Grand Duchy of Tuscany. Since Dante, Tuscan—and specifically the dialect of Florence—had become a literary language for writers not necessarily from Tuscany. It was also a means of communication for the educated elites of the various states into which the Italian peninsula had been divided, much in the way that people from different countries in Europe today use English as their common language.

But precisely what kind of Tuscan should be used in the future, unified Italy was a subject of debate: the language of its literati was different from the everyday dialect spoken by Tuscans. Collodi, himself a Tuscan, was closely involved in that debate, as a member of the board that the government of the day appointed for the preparation of an authoritative dictionary of Italian, the *Novo vocabolario della lingua italiana secondo l'uso di Firenze* (New Dictionary of the Italian Language according to the Usage of Florence). Collodi favored a more colloquial variant than that endorsed by the venerable Acca-

demia della Crusca, which had been founded in the late sixteenth century and whose members had come to be regarded
as the guardians of linguistic orthodoxy. It was in this context
that he wrote the *Adventures*, introducing into his narrative
phrasings and nuances that are hard to appreciate fully without the cultural and linguistic sensibility that comes with
being a Florentine-born Tuscan. Our translation has benefited
greatly from the fact that one of us is.

Pinocchio speaks a correct but informal Italian that we have
tried to reflect by dropping into his speech casual-sounding
words and phrases, while at the same time avoiding outright
slang. Thus, in chapter 17, he does not pretend to be "annoyed,"
"disturbed," or "vexed" by the pillow at his feet, but "bugged"
by it.

Much else that characterizes Collodi's masterpiece has in-
evitably been sacrificed in the transition from one language to
another. Puns, obviously. But also the extensive use of suffixes
in Italian to add color to a noun in a way that is possible in
English only with the use of an adjective—and sometimes even
two. When, for example, Pinocchio goes to town to beg and
Collodi describes the hat that he proffers as a *cappelluccio*, he
is telling his readers that it is not only small but also of poor
quality. To convey both concepts, we used "pitiful little hat,"
but we would be the first to admit that it lacks the concise impact of the original.

Also lost in translation to English are the dynamics of personal interaction that an Italian-language reader instinctively
grasps, according to which form of "you" is being used. There
are three: *tu*, *voi*, and *lei*. Each makes clear exactly what kind
of rapport exists between the characters. And sometimes, as
their relationship changes, so does the pronoun.

As two craftsmen, Geppetto and Mr. Cherry address each
other respectfully as *voi*. But when they fight, they switch to
the familiar *tu*, and when they make up, they switch back to
voi. Pinocchio, while still a mischievous spirit trapped in a
piece of wood, speaks to Mr. Cherry in the informal *tu* form.
But the moment he begins to talk to his creator, Geppetto, he
uses the more formal *voi*, which is how children in late

nineteenth-century Italy addressed their parents. In the same way, while the Fairy is a little girl, the puppet treats her as an equal, using *tu*. But as soon as she adopts the behavior of a mother, he adopts *voi*. Yet more formal than *voi* in Collodi's time was the pronoun *lei*, which has since become the respectful form throughout the north and center of Italy while *voi* remains common in the south. *Lei* crops up only rarely in the *Adventures*, but when Pinocchio is brought face-to-face with the monstrous Fire-Eater, he swiftly—and wisely—addresses him using the *lei* form.

Collodi also scattered throughout his story Tuscan dialect terms such as *babbo* for "father" and grammatical idiosyncrasies such as *gli è* for "it is" or "he is." But, sadly, no amount of verbal inventiveness can reproduce for an English-language reader the often humorous effect these *toscanismi* had—and still have—on Italians.

One of the thorniest challenges facing translators of the *Adventures* is posed by a single concept, but one that is crucial to the narrative. It is expressed by the words *perbene* (also written *per bene*) and *ammodo*. Collodi uses them to weave a thread that runs through the story from the very "birth" of Pinocchio to the closing scene in which he gives the concept even greater importance by choosing *perbene* as the word with which to end his book. *Perbene* and *ammodo* encompass a broad spectrum of meaning. At one end, they have roughly the same meaning as "respectable." At the other end, they can mean simply "good" or "decent." When today's Italians talk of *una persona perbene*, they could be referring to someone who is an upright citizen or just a good person. As early as chapter 3, Geppetto voices the seemingly forlorn hope that Pinocchio should be *un burattino per bene*. The Blue-haired Fairy, the puppet's other "parent," later expresses a similar wish: that he should become *un ragazzino perbene*.

One possible translation is "proper." But it suffers from two shortcomings. The first is that, while reflecting the idea of social conformity, it conveys to only a limited extent that of moral integrity. More awkwardly, "proper" itself has more than one meaning in English. It can denote not only "respectable," but also "real," "authentic," "genuine"—and that has a direct bearing on Collodi's narrative. While Pinocchio's parents, and latterly the puppet himself, all aspire to his becoming *perbene* in the sense of well-behaved and socially responsible, the puppet wants to become a real boy—a human, rather than a marionette. The two concepts are entwined—as the Fairy explains, he needs to become *perbene* before he can become human—but are nevertheless distinct. Using "proper," as in "a proper boy," conflates and confuses the two concepts. We therefore opted to use "good" (or "good little") boy or kid, depending on the context. Only where *perbene* evidently refers to social propriety have we used "respectable" instead.

We wish to extend special thanks to Dr. Bianca Finzi-Contini Calabresi of Columbia University for helping to guide us along the sometimes ill-defined frontier that separates British from American English; to Maria Cristina Anzilotti of the Fondazione Nazionale Carlo Collodi for her wholehearted encouragement of our project; to Andrew Stuart, our agent, for his persistence and enthusiasm; and to John Siciliano of Penguin Classics, who embraced our vision of an annotated version of *The Adventures of Pinocchio* that would show Collodi's story was—and is—more than just "kids' stuff."

The Adventures of
Pinocchio

How it happened that Mr. Cherry, a carpenter, found a piece of wood that cried and laughed like a child.

Once upon a time[1] there was . . .

"A king!" my little readers will no doubt say in a flash.

"No, kids. You got it wrong. Once upon a time there was . . . a piece of wood."[2]

It wasn't a fancy piece of wood: just an ordinary log from a stack,[3] the kind you use for stoves and fireplaces to heat rooms in winter.

I don't know how it happened, but the fact is that one fine day this piece of wood happened to turn up in the workshop of an old carpenter. His name was Master[4] Antonio, but everybody called him Mr.[5] Cherry, because the tip of his nose was always shiny and deep red, like a ripe cherry.

No sooner had Mr. Cherry caught sight of that piece of wood than he brightened up and, rubbing his hands together in delight, muttered to himself under his breath:

"This piece of wood turned up at just the right moment: I want to use it to make a little table leg."[6]

Without further ado, he picked up his sharpened adze[7] to start stripping away the bark and to cut down the piece of wood, but when he was about to strike the first blow, he froze with his arm in the air because he heard a tiny little voice say imploringly:

"Don't hit me too hard!"

Imagine old Mr. Cherry's reaction! His bewildered eyes roved around the room to see where on earth that little voice could have come from. But there was no one there! He looked under the workbench . . . no one there. He looked inside a wardrobe that was always kept shut . . . no one there; he looked inside the basket for wood shavings and sawdust . . . no one there. He even opened the workshop door to look down the street . . . no one there! So then?

"I get it," he said, laughing and scratching his wig.[8] "I guess that little voice—it was just my imagination. Back to work!"

And with the adze in his hand again, he let fly an unholy blow at the piece of wood.

"Ow! That hurt!" cried the same little voice in a reproachful tone.

This time Mr. Cherry turned to stone, his eyes bulging out of his head in fear, his mouth wide open, and his tongue hanging down to his chin like a gargoyle on a fountain.

As soon as he was able to speak again, he started to say, trembling and stuttering from the shock: "But where could it have come from—that little voice that said 'Ow'? . . . There's not a living soul here! Could it possibly be that this piece of wood has learned to cry and moan like a child? I don't believe that. This piece of wood—here it is—this is a piece of wood for the fireplace, like all the others, and if it were thrown on the fire, it'd do for boiling a pot of beans.[9] . . . So then? Could there be someone hiding inside it? If there *is* someone hiding inside, he'll be sorry. I'll fix him!"

So saying, he grabbed the poor piece of wood with both hands and set about smashing it unmercifully against the walls of the room.

Then he stopped to listen—to hear if some little voice was complaining. He waited for two minutes . . . nothing; five minutes . . . nothing; ten minutes . . . nothing!

"I see," he said, making an effort to laugh and ruffling his wig. "I suppose that little voice that said 'Ow'—well, it was just my imagination. Let's get back to work."

And because fear had really taken hold of him, he tried to sing a little to give himself courage.

Meanwhile, with his adze set to one side, he took up his plane to smooth the piece of wood. But while he was planing back and forth, he heard the same little voice, which said to him with a laugh:

"Stop it! You're tickling my belly."[10]

This time, poor Mr. Cherry fell over as if he had been struck by lightning. When he opened his eyes again, he found himself sitting on the ground.

His face seemed to have been transformed. Even the tip of his nose—usually so red—had gone blue with terror.

*Mr. Cherry gives the piece of wood as
a present to his friend Geppetto, who takes
it to make himself a wonderful puppet
that can dance, fence, and do flips.*

Just then, there came a knock at the door.

"Come on in," said the carpenter, without having the strength to pull himself up.

In came a sprightly little old man whose name was Geppetto.[11] But the neighborhood kids, when they wanted to drive him into a fury, would call him by a nickname—Cornmush, on account of his yellow wig that looked so much like mushy cornmeal.[12]

Geppetto had a hair-trigger temper. You'd better watch out if you called him Cornmush! He would instantly go wild, and there was no way of holding him back.

"Good morning, Master Antonio," said Geppetto. "What are you doing down there on the floor?"

"I'm teaching ants to do math."

"Much good may it do you!"

"What has brought you here, Geppetto my old friend?"

"My own legs. You see, Master Antonio, I've come here to ask you a favor."

"Well, here I am. How can I be of service to you?" said the carpenter, pulling himself up onto his knees.

"This morning I had a brainstorm."

"Let's hear about it."

"I thought of making myself—all on my own—a nice wooden

puppet,[13] but a *wonderful* puppet, one that can dance, and fence, and do flips. I want to go around the world with this puppet, and earn myself a crust of bread and a glass of wine.[14] What do you think?"

"Good for you, Cornmush!" shouted the same little voice[15]— but it was impossible to figure out where it came from.

Hearing himself called Cornmush, old Geppetto got so furious that he turned as red as a hot pepper and, turning on the carpenter, asked him, wild with rage:

"Why are you calling me names?"

"Who's calling you names?"

"You called me Cornmush! . . ."

"It wasn't me!"

"So then it was *me*? I say it was *you*!"

"No!"

"Yes!"

"No."

"Yes."

And as they got more and more heated, they turned from words to deeds and, grabbing hold of each other, they scratched, they bit, and roughed each other up.

Once the battle was over, Master Antonio found himself with Geppetto's yellow wig in his hands, and Geppetto realized he had the carpenter's salt-and-pepper one in his mouth!

"Give me back my wig!" shouted Master Antonio.

"And you give me back mine, and let's make up."

The two little old men, after having each taken back their own wig, shook hands and swore to remain good friends to the end of their days.

"So, Geppetto my old friend," said the carpenter, to show that they had made peace, "what's the favor you'd like of me?"

"I'd like a piece of wood to make my puppet. Will you give me one?"

Master Antonio, as happy as could be, went to his counter to get the piece of wood that had scared him so badly. But just as he was about to hand it to his friend, the piece of wood gave a yank, wriggled violently out of his hands, and slammed fiercely into poor Geppetto's shriveled-up, bony shins.[16]

"Ouch! Is this the care, Master Antonio, with which you give me your stuff as a present? You almost crippled me! . . ."

"I swear it wasn't me!"

"So then it was me! . . ."

"It's all this piece of wood's fault . . ."

"I know it's the wood's fault: but it was you who hit me with it on the legs!"

"I didn't!"

"Liar!"

"Geppetto, don't call me names, or I'll call you Cornmush! . . ."

"Donkey!"

"Cornmush!"

"Jackass"

"Cornmush!"

"You ugly little monkey!"

"Cornmush!"

Hearing himself called Cornmush for the third time, Geppetto lost it. He flung himself onto the carpenter, and they gave each other a good clobbering.

When the battle was over, Master Antonio ended up with two more scratches on his nose, and the other with two buttons fewer on his jacket. With the score evened up this way, they shook hands and swore to remain good friends to the end of their days.

Meanwhile, Geppetto took his nice[17] piece of wood and, thanking Master Antonio, went back home limping.

Back at home, Geppetto immediately starts making himself the puppet and names it Pinocchio. The puppet's first mischief.

Geppetto's home was a little ground-floor room that got its light from a space under the stairs.[18] The furniture could not have been more basic: a worn-out chair, a crummy bed, and a totally derelict little table. At the far end of the room you could see a fireplace with a fire going; but the fire had been painted, and next to it was a painted pot that was boiling away merrily. It gave off a cloud of steam that looked real.

As soon as he got home, Geppetto picked up his tools and set himself to carving and making his puppet.

"What name will I give him?" he said to himself. "I want to call him Pinocchio.[19] That'll bring him good luck. I once met a whole family of Pinocchios: Pinocchio was the father's name, Pinocchia the mother's name, and the kids too were Pinocchios. They all got on pretty well in life. The richest of them was a beggar."[20]

Once he had found a name for his puppet, Geppetto got to work with a vengeance, first making the hair, then the forehead, and then the eyes.

When the eyes were finished, just imagine Geppetto's astonishment when he realized they were moving and had fixed a steady, unflinching gaze on him.

Geppetto, seeing himself watched by those two wooden eyes, felt almost offended and said in a resentful tone:

"You pesky wooden eyes, why are you looking at me?"

No one answered.

So, after the eyes, he made the nose. But the nose, as soon as it was made, began to grow. And it grew, and grew, and grew—until in a few minutes it became a big, long nose that had no end.

Poor old Geppetto was having a hard time cutting it back, because the more he tried to shorten it, the longer that impertinent nose grew.[21]

After the nose, he made the mouth.

The mouth had not even been finished when it started laughing and making fun of him.

"Stop that laughing!" said Geppetto resentfully. But it was like talking to a brick wall.

"I said, stop that laughing!" he shouted in a threatening voice.

So the mouth stopped laughing, but stuck its tongue all the way out.

Geppetto, so as not to spoil his mood, pretended he hadn't noticed, and kept on working. After the mouth, he made the chin, then the neck, then the shoulders, then the stomach, the arms, and the hands.

As soon as he had completed the hands, Geppetto felt his wig being lifted off his head. He looked up, and what did he see? His yellow wig in the puppet's hands.

"Pinocchio! . . . Give me back my wig this instant!"

But Pinocchio, instead of giving back the wig, put it on his own head so that he was half-smothered under it.

Faced with this insolent and derisive behavior, Geppetto became sad and melancholy—more so than he had ever been in his life. And, turning to Pinocchio, he said:

"You naughty child! You're still not finished being made, and already you're beginning to treat your father with disrespect! Bad, my boy—very bad!"

And he wiped away a tear.

The legs and feet still had to be made.

When Geppetto had finished making the feet, he felt a kick on the tip of his nose.

"I deserve it!" he muttered to himself. "I should have known what I was getting myself into! It's too late now!"

Then he took the puppet under its arms and set it down on the ground, onto the floor of the room,[22] to make it walk.

Pinocchio's legs were all stiff and he didn't know how to move. Geppetto led him by the hand to teach him how to put one foot in front of the other.

When his legs had loosened up, Pinocchio started to walk on his own and run around the room until, slipping out through the front door, he leapt into the street and began to run away.

And there poor Geppetto was, running after him, unable to catch up with him because that naughty little Pinocchio was leaping ahead like a hare, his wooden feet clattering on the paving stones, making a racket like twenty pairs of farmers' clogs.[23]

"Catch him! Catch him!" Geppetto was shouting. But the people on the street, seeing this wooden puppet racing along like a thoroughbred, would stop to marvel at him, and laugh and laugh and laugh—so hard you cannot imagine.

In the end, and by good fortune, it just so happened that a Carabiniere[24] was passing by. Hearing all the commotion, and believing it was a colt that had gotten free from its owner, he planted himself courageously in the middle of the road with his legs astride, and with the firm intention of stopping it and avoiding any greater calamity.

But Pinocchio saw from a distance that the Carabiniere was there, blocking the entire street, and figured he would trick him by slipping between his legs to get past. Instead, he blew it.

Without budging an inch, the Carabiniere caught him cleanly by the nose (it was an exaggeratedly long nose, which seemed made for the very purpose of being seized by Carabinieri) and delivered him back into Geppetto's hands. To instill some discipline into Pinocchio, Geppetto wanted to give him a good tug on the ears. But just imagine the look on his face when he felt for the ears and couldn't find them. And you know why? Because in his hurry to carve the puppet, he had forgotten to make them.

So he took Pinocchio by the scruff of his neck and, as he was taking him back, told him, with a menacing shake of his head:

"We're going straight home. When we get there, you can be sure there'll be a reckoning!"

Pinocchio, catching Geppetto's drift, threw himself on the ground and refused to walk any farther. Meanwhile, the curious and the idle clustered together in small groups to watch.

Some would say one thing, some another.

"Poor puppet!" some said. "He's right not to want to go home! Who knows how that awful man Geppetto might beat him! . . ."

And others added maliciously:

"That Geppetto looks like a good man! But he's a real tyrant with kids! If they leave that poor puppet in his hands, he's perfectly capable of busting him to pieces . . ."

Such was the fuss that in the end the Carabiniere set Pinocchio free again and led Geppetto—that poor man—to prison. At a loss for words to defend himself, Geppetto was weeping like a little calf. As he headed to jail, he blabbered, sobbing:

"Wretched son! And to think I went through so much trouble to make him a good little puppet! But it serves me right! I should have known what I was getting myself into! . . ."

What happened afterward is a story that defies belief, and I shall tell it to you in the chapters that follow.

*The story of Pinocchio and the
Talking Cricket, in which you can see how
bad kids don't like to be corrected by those
who know more than they do.*

I will tell you, then, kids, that while poor Geppetto was being led away to prison through no fault of his own, that little scoundrel Pinocchio, freed from the Carabiniere's clutches, was running like mad through the fields to get himself home as soon as possible. And as he ran, in his hurry he jumped over lofty embankments, bramble hedges, and ditches full of water, just like a little goat or a young hare pursued by hunters.

Once he reached home, he found that the front door was ajar. He pushed it and went in. As soon as he had secured it with the latch, he threw himself onto the ground and, sitting there, let out a great big sigh of contentment.

But the contentment didn't last long, because he heard someone in the room going:

"Chirp-chirp-chirp!"

"Who's that calling me?" said Pinocchio, as spooked as could be.

"It's me!"

Pinocchio turned around and saw a big cricket[25] that was slowly climbing up the wall.

"Tell me, Cricket, who are you?"

"I'm the Talking Cricket, and I've been living in this room for more than a hundred years."

"But today this room belongs to me," said the puppet. "And

if you really want to do me a favor, get lost—right now! And don't even look back."

"I'm not leaving this place," answered the Cricket, "until I've told you a great truth."

"Just tell me, and make it quick."

"Terrible things happen to children who rebel against their parents and capriciously run away from their father's home.[26] They will never come to any good in this world, and sooner or later they will bitterly regret it."

"Chirp on, my dear Cricket, just as much as you want: but I know that tomorrow at dawn, I want to leave this place, because if I stay here, what happens to all kids is going to happen to me too—they're going to send me to school, and whether I like it or not I'm going to have to study. And between us, I really don't feel a bit like studying, because I get lots more fun out of chasing butterflies and climbing trees to catch little birds in their nests."

"You poor little sucker! Don't you know that, by acting that way, you're bound to grow up to be an absolute donkey and that everyone will make a fool out of you?"[27]

"Shut up, you awful, gloomy Cricket!" shouted Pinocchio.

But instead of feeling hurt by this insolent reply, the Cricket, who was patient and philosophical, continued in the same tone of voice:

"And if it doesn't suit you to go to school, why don't you at least learn a trade, so you can earn an honest living?"

"You want me to tell you why?" replied Pinocchio, who was starting to lose his patience. "Of all the trades in the world, there's only one I really go for."

"And what would that be?"

"Eating, drinking, sleeping, having fun, and living from morning to night like a drifter."

"For your information," said the Talking Cricket with his usual calm, "all those who are in that trade almost always end up in the poorhouse or jail."

"I'm warning you, you awful, gloomy Cricket . . . ! If I get mad, you'd better watch out!"

"Poor Pinocchio! I really feel sorry for you! . . ."

"Why do you feel sorry for me?"

"Because you're a puppet, and what's worse, your head is made of wood."

At these words, Pinocchio sprang to his feet in a fury and, seizing a wooden mallet from the counter, flung it at the Talking Cricket.

Maybe he didn't even mean to hit him. But unfortunately it just so happened he got him right on the head. So the poor Cricket had barely enough breath to go *"chirp-chirp-chirp"* and then was left there—stone dead, stuck to the wall.

Pinocchio is hungry and looks for an egg to make himself an omelet; but just as he's about to cook it, the omelet flies out the window.

Meanwhile, it was starting to get dark, and Pinocchio, remembering that he hadn't eaten, realized he had an unpleasant sensation in his stomach that felt a lot like an appetite.

But kids' appetites grow quickly, and, in fact, after just a few minutes, the appetite turned into hunger. And in a flash, the hunger turned into a ravenous hunger—a hunger so real it could be cut with a knife.

Poor Pinocchio ran straight to the fireplace, where a pot was boiling, and was about to take the lid off to see what was inside. But the pot was only painted on the wall. Just imagine his disappointment. His nose, which was already long to begin with, grew the width of at least four fingers.[28]

At that point he started running around the room, rummaging through every drawer and closet in search of some bread—maybe even some stale bread, a tiny crust, a bone left over from the dog, a bit of moldy polenta, a fishbone, a cherry pit, something at least to chew on. But he found nothing—a great big nothing. Truly nothing.

And meanwhile his hunger was growing, and it kept on growing, and the only relief poor Pinocchio could find was to yawn. And he was producing such immense yawns that sometimes his mouth would reach his ears.[29] And having yawned, he would spit, and would feel his stomach shrinking—to nothing.

So, weeping and flying into a screaming temper, he said:

"The Talking Cricket was right. I did the wrong thing rebelling against my dad[30] and running away from home . . . If my dad were here, now I wouldn't find myself dying of yawns! Oh, hunger is such a terrible illness!"

Then all of a sudden he thought he saw, in the garbage pile, something round and white that looked very much like a hen's egg. In a single movement, he leapt up and threw himself on it. It really *was* an egg.

It's impossible to describe the puppet's joy: you've just got to be able to picture it. Almost thinking it was a dream, he kept turning the egg over in his hands, touching it and kissing it. And as he kissed it, he said:

"Now how shall I prepare it? Shall I make an omelet? No, it's better to cook it in a dish. But wouldn't it be tastier if I fried it in a pan? Or if instead I cooked it so as to drink it?[31] No, the quickest way of all is to cook it in a dish or a skillet: I just can't wait to eat it!"

No sooner said than done, he put a little skillet on a brazier full of hot coals: in the skillet, instead of oil or butter, he put some water, and when the water began to give off steam— crack! . . . he broke the shell and was about to put the egg in.

But instead of the white and the yolk, a little chick popped out, as cheerful and gracious as could be, and bowing respectfully it said:

"Many thanks, Mister Pinocchio, for having spared me the work of breaking the shell! See you again, take care, and many greetings to your family!"

That said, the chick spread its wings and, slipping through the open window, flew off into the distance.

The poor puppet was left there, as if under a spell, with his eyes staring, his mouth open, and the eggshell in his hand. Then, once he had recovered from his initial bewilderment, he started to cry and scream and stomp his feet in desperation, and as he cried, he said:

"The Talking Cricket was right! If I hadn't run away from home and if my dad were here, now I wouldn't find myself dying of hunger! . . . Oh, hunger is such a terrible illness! . . ."

And since his stomach kept on rumbling more than ever, and he didn't know how to make it shut up, he thought of going out to pay a quick visit to the small town nearby in the hope of finding some charitable person who might give him a handout of a little bit of bread.

6

Pinocchio falls asleep with his feet on the
brazier, and the next morning he wakes
up with his feet all burnt.

It just so happened that it was a foul and hellish night. Thunder was roaring loud and strong. Lightning was flashing as if the sky were catching fire. And a cold, biting, unruly wind, hissing and raising an immense cloud of dust, made all the trees in the countryside screech and creak.

Pinocchio was really scared of thunder and lightning. But his hunger was stronger than his fear. So, closing the front door only partially, and launching himself on his way, he reached the town in about a hundred leaps, panting and with his tongue hanging out, just like a hunting dog.

But he found that everything was dark and deserted. The stores were closed. Front doors were shut. Windows were shut. And in the street—not even a dog. It seemed like the land of the dead.

So Pinocchio, seized by hunger and desperation, grabbed hold of a doorbell[32] and began to ring it incessantly, saying to himself:

"Someone is bound to look out the window."

Sure enough, a little old man with his nightcap on appeared in a window and shouted irascibly:

"What do you want at this time of night?"

"Hey, could you do me a favor and give me some bread?"

"Wait for me there and I'll be right back," answered the little old man, thinking he was dealing with one of those trouble-making kids who get a kick out of ringing doorbells in the middle of the night to harass respectable folk while they're enjoying a peaceful night's sleep.

After half a minute the window opened again, and the same little old man's voice shouted to Pinocchio:

"Come under here and hold out your hat."

Pinocchio immediately took off his pitiful little hat. But as he was about to hold it out, he felt an enormous basinful of water pour down on him. It drenched him from head to foot, as if he had been a pot with a wilted geranium in it.

He returned home as soaked as a drowned rat, beat by hunger and exhaustion. And since he no longer had the strength to stand upright, he sat down and rested his sodden, mud-spattered feet on a brazier full of hot coals.

And there he fell asleep. But as he slept, his wooden feet caught fire. Little by little they turned into charcoal and then to ashes.

But Pinocchio kept on sleeping and snoring—as if his feet belonged to someone else. Finally, at the break of day, he woke up, because someone had knocked at the door.

"Who is it?" he asked, yawning and rubbing his eyes.

"It's me," answered a voice.

It was the voice of Geppetto.

7

Geppetto comes home, remakes the puppet's feet and gives him the breakfast that the poor man had brought back for himself.

Pinocchio, who was still lost in sleep, hadn't yet noticed that his feet were completely burned. So, as soon as he heard his father's voice, he leapt off the stool to run and unlatch the door. But instead, after swaying two or three times, he fell flat on the ground.

Hitting the floor, he made the same noise that a bunch of wooden spoons dropped from the fifth floor would have made.

"Open up!" Geppetto continued to shout from out in the street.

"My dear dad, I can't," the puppet replied, crying and rolling over on the ground.

"Why can't you?"

"Because they ate my feet."

"*Who* ate your feet?"

"The cat did,"[33] said Pinocchio, seeing the cat, which was having fun making some wood shavings dance around with its front paws.[34]

"Open up, I say!" repeated Geppetto, "otherwise when I get inside, I'll give you 'cat'!"

"I can't stand up. Believe me. Oh, poor me! Poor me! I'll have to walk on my knees for the rest of my life! . . ."

Geppetto, thinking that all this fuss was just Pinocchio causing trouble again, decided to put a stop to it. He climbed up the wall and entered the house through the window.

At first he had all sorts of things in mind. But then, when he saw his Pinocchio lying flat on the ground and *really* with no feet—well, then he felt his heart grow tender, and picking him up in his arms, he started kissing him and giving him thousands of cuddles and murmuring thousands of endearments. With great big tears running down his cheeks, he said to him, sobbing:

"My sweet little Pinocchio! How is it that you burned your feet?"

"I don't know, Dad, but believe me, it was a hellish night, and I'll remember it for as long as I live. The thunder was roaring and the lightning was flashing, and I was so hungry and then the Talking Cricket said, 'It serves you right: you were bad and you deserve it,' and I said to him, 'Watch out, Cricket! . . .' and he said, 'You're a puppet and your head is made of wood,' and I threw the handle of a mallet at him, and he died, but it was his own fault, because I didn't want to kill him, which can be proved by the fact that I put a little skillet on the hot coals of the brazier, but the chick popped out and said, 'See you again and many greetings to your family,' and my hunger kept on growing, which is why that little old man in a nightcap, looking out the window, said to me, 'Come under here and hold your hat out.' And me? With that basinful of water on my head—because to ask for a little bit of bread is no shame, is it?—I came straight back home, and because I was still so hungry I put my feet on the brazier to get myself dry, and you came back, and I found them burnt, and meanwhile my hunger is still here but my feet no longer are! *Boo-hoo-hoo! . . . Boo-hoo-hoo! . . .*"

And poor Pinocchio started crying and bawling so loud he could be heard from three miles away.

Geppetto, who had understood only one thing from that whole garbled account, which was that the puppet was starving to death, pulled three pears out of his pocket and, handing them to Pinocchio, said:

"These three pears were for my breakfast, but I'll happily give them to you. Eat them, and I hope they do you good."

"If you want me to eat them, do me the favor of peeling them."

"Of *peeling* them?" replied Geppetto, astonished. "I never would have thought, my dear boy, that you were so finicky and fastidious in your eating. That's a bad thing! In this world, from the time we're children, we have to get used to not picking and choosing—and eating everything, because we never know what fate can befall us. Anything can happen! . . ."

"You may be right," replied Pinocchio. "But me? I'll never eat a piece of fruit that isn't peeled. I can't stand the skin."

So that good man Geppetto pulled out a little knife and, armed with great patience, peeled the three pears and put all the peels on the corner of the table.

When Pinocchio had eaten the first pear in two bites, he was about to throw the core away, but Geppetto took hold of his arm and said:

"Don't throw it away: everything in this world can come in handy."

"But I'm certainly not going to eat the core! . . ." cried the puppet, snapping back at him like a viper.

"Who knows? Anything can happen! . . ." Geppetto repeated without losing his composure.

In any case, the three cores, instead of being thrown out the window, were put on the corner of the table together with the peels.

Once the pears were eaten—or rather devoured—Pinocchio gave a long yawn and said, in a whining voice:

"I'm still hungry!"

"But, my dear boy, I have nothing else to give you."

"You mean nothing—really *nothing*?"

"All I have is these peels and these three pear cores."

"Oh well!"[35] said Pinocchio. "If there's nothing else, I'll eat a peel."

And he started chewing. At first he made a face, but then, in a flash, he gobbled up all the peels one after another. And after the peels, the cores too. And when he had finished eating everything, he patted his belly with his hands and said gloatingly:

"Now I sure feel good!"

"So you see," said Geppetto, "I was right when I told you we mustn't be too finicky or dainty in our eating. My dear boy, we never know what fate can befall us in this world. Anything can happen! . . ."[36]

*Geppetto remakes Pinocchio's feet and sells his
own coat to buy him a spelling book.*

As soon as he was no longer hungry, the puppet started grip-
ing and crying because he wanted a new pair of feet.

But Geppetto, to punish him for being so naughty, let him
cry and drown in despair for half a day. Then he said:

"So why should I remake your feet? So you can run away
from home again?"

"I promise you," said the puppet, sobbing, "that as of today
I'll be good . . ."

"All kids," replied Geppetto, "when they want to get their
way, say that."

"I promise you. I'll go to school.³⁷ I'll study and I'll do myself proud . . ."

"All kids, when they want to get their way, repeat the same
old thing."

"But I'm not like other kids! I'm better than all of them, and
I always tell the truth. I promise you, Dad, that I'll learn a
trade and stand by you and take care of you in your old age."

Although Geppetto was wearing the expression of a tyrant,
he felt like crying and his heart was swollen with compassion
from seeing his poor Pinocchio in that pitiful state. He said no
more, and, picking up the tools of his trade and two little pieces
of aged wood, he set to work with total dedication.

In less than an hour, the feet were all nice and finished—
two slender, nervous, quick little feet, as if shaped by an artist
of genius.

At that point Geppetto said to the puppet:

"Close your eyes and go to sleep!"

So Pinocchio closed his eyes and pretended to sleep. And while he was pretending to be asleep, Geppetto, using some glue diluted in an eggshell, stuck Pinocchio's feet back where they belonged, and stuck them back on so well you couldn't even see the point at which they had been attached.

As soon as the puppet realized he had his feet again, he jumped down from the table he was lying on and started skipping and performing all sorts of flips, as if crazy with joy.

"To reward you for what you've done for me," Pinocchio said to his dad, "I want to go to school right away."

"Good boy."

"But in order to go to school, I need clothes."

So Geppetto, who was poor and didn't have a cent on him, made Pinocchio a meager little outfit from flowered paper, a pair of shoes from tree bark, and a little hat[38] from the soft part of a piece of bread.

Pinocchio ran to look at himself in a basin full of water and was so happy with himself that he strutted around like a peacock:

"I sure look like a gentleman!"

"That's right," replied Geppetto, "because—bear this in mind—it's not the good-looking suit that makes the gentleman, but rather the clean one."

"Speaking of that," said the puppet, "in order to go to school, there's something I still don't have—in fact, I still don't have the most essential and important thing."

"Which is?"

"I don't have a spelling book."

"You're right. But how do we get one?"

"Very simple: we go to a bookshop and buy one."

"And what about the money?"[39]

"I don't have any."

"Neither do I," added the good old man, becoming dejected.

And though Pinocchio was a very cheerful boy, he too became dejected: because when poverty is truly poverty, everyone—even kids—understand it.

"Oh well!" cried Geppetto, standing up all of a sudden. He

put on his old moleskin coat,[40] which was all patches and repairs, and ran out of the house.

After a while he came back, and when he did, he was holding the boy's spelling book. But he was no longer wearing his coat. The poor man was in his shirtsleeves. And it was snowing outside.

"What about your coat, Dad?"

"I sold it."

"And why did you sell it?"

"Because I was too hot in it."

Pinocchio immediately understood Geppetto's reply, and, unable to restrain the impulse of his good heart, he flung himself into Geppetto's arms and, holding him around his neck, began to kiss him all over his face.

*Pinocchio sells the spelling book to go
see a show at the puppet theater.*

Once it had stopped snowing, Pinocchio, his nice spelling book under his arm, took the road that led to the school, and on the way, a thousand thoughts and pipe dreams were taking shape and whirling around in his brain—each one more wondrous than the other.

And having a conversation with himself, he said:

"The first thing I want to learn in school today is how to read. Then tomorrow I'll learn how to write. And the day after tomorrow I'll learn to do numbers. Then with my skills I'll earn loads of cash, and with the first cash that comes into my pocket, I want to get my dad a nice woolen coat. What am I saying—woolen? I want to get it all made up in silver and gold, with buttons made of diamonds. That poor man really deserves it, because—come on!—to buy me my books and get me an education, he was left in his shirtsleeves . . . in this cold weather! Only dads are willing to make those kinds of sacrifices! . . ."

While he was saying these things, his heart swollen with emotion, he thought he heard from a distance the music of fifes and a big drum: *phee-phee-phee, phee-phee-phee, zum, zum, zum, zum.*

He stopped and listened. The sounds were coming from the far end of a very long side street that led to a tiny little village on the seashore.

"I wonder what that music is? What a shame I have to go to school, otherwise . . ."

And he just stood there, filled with doubts. In any case, a decision had to be made: either go to school or listen to the fifes.

"Today I'll go listen to the fifes, and tomorrow, school. There's always time to go to school," said the little rascal at last, with a shrug of his shoulders.

No sooner said than done, he slipped down the side street and started running like crazy. The more he ran the more he could make out the sound of the fifes and the thudding of the big drum: *phee-phee-phee, phee-phee-phee, phee-phee-phee, zum, zum, zum, zum.*

Then all of a sudden he found himself in the middle of a piazza full of people who were all crowding around a great big makeshift structure of wood and canvas that was painted a myriad of colors.

"What's that?" Pinocchio asked, turning to a little kid who was from the town.

"Read the sign that's written there and you'll know."

"I'd be happy to read it, but it just so happens that today I don't know how to read."

"Good job—you dimwit." Then I'll read it to you. So listen up—on that sign it says, in flaming red letters, GRAND PUPPET THEATER . . ."

"Has the show been going on for long?"

"It's starting now."

"And how much does it cost to get in?"

"Four *soldi*."[41] Pinocchio, who was in a fever of curiosity, lost all self-control and with no shame whatsoever said to the little kid:

"Would you give me four *soldi* until tomorrow?"

"I'd be happy to give them to you," replied the kid, making fun of him. "But it just so happens that today I can't."

"For four *soldi*, I'll sell you my little jacket," the puppet replied.

"What do you want me to do with your little flowered paper jacket? If it gets rained on, there'll be no way to even get it off."

"Do you want to buy my shoes?"

"They're good for lighting a fire."

"How much will you give me for my hat?"

"A great purchase that would be! A hat made of bread! I'd be in danger of mice coming and eating it off my head!"

Pinocchio was on pins and needles. He was about to make a last offer. But he couldn't summon the courage. He was hesitating, wavering, suffering. Finally, he said:

"Will you give me four *soldi* for this new spelling book?"

"I'm a kid and I don't buy stuff from kids," replied the other boy, who had much better judgment than Pinocchio.

"For four *soldi I'll* buy the spelling book," cried a used clothes salesman who had been witness to the conversation.

So the book was sold then and there. And to think that that poor man Geppetto was back home, shivering from the cold in his shirtsleeves because he had bought his boy that spelling book!

*The puppets recognize their brother Pinocchio
and go wild over him, but just when things
are getting really fun, the puppeteer Fire-eater
comes out, and Pinocchio risks coming to
a bad end.*

When Pinocchio entered the marionette theater, something happened that sparked a sort of revolution.

The stage curtain had been pulled up, you see, and the show had already begun.

On the stage you could see Harlequin and Pulcinella, who were bickering with each other and, as usual, threatening to exchange a flurry of slaps and blows from one moment to the next.

The audience was riveted to the scene. Everyone was splitting their sides laughing as they listened to the squabble. The two puppets were inventing and trading all sorts of insults as realistically as if they had truly been two rational creatures of this world.

Then, all of a sudden and without any warning, Harlequin stops playing his part and, turning toward the audience and pointing to someone in the seats at the back, cries out dramatically:

"Good heavens above! Am I awake or am I dreaming? Because that guy down there is Pinocchio! . . ."

"It really *is* Pinocchio!" shouts Pulcinella.

"It's him all right," yells Signora Rosaura, poking her head out from the back of the stage.

"It's Pinocchio! It's Pinocchio," all the puppets shout in unison, jumping out from the wings. "It's Pinocchio! It's our brother Pinocchio! Hooray for Pinocchio!"

"Pinocchio, come up here with me," shouts Harlequin. "Come and throw yourself into the arms of your wooden brothers and sisters!"

At this affectionate invitation, Pinocchio bounds up into the air, and from the seats at the rear he reaches the more exclusive ones at the front, and with another leap from the exclusive seats, he steps onto the conductor's head and from there onto the stage.[42]

You cannot imagine the hugs, the neck squeezes, the friendly pinches and the butting of heads in true and sincere brother-and-sisterhood that Pinocchio received in the midst of such confusion, all stirred up by the actors and actresses in that company of ligneous thespians.

It was a moving thing to see—no doubt about it. But the theater audience, seeing that the show had come to a halt, lost patience and started shouting: "We want the comedy! We want the comedy!"

All wasted breath, because instead of continuing with the show, the puppets redoubled the racket and the shouting, and putting Pinocchio on their shoulders, they carried him triumphantly into the limelight.

At that point, the puppeteer came out—a big man so hideous you'd get scared just by looking at him. He had an ugly beard as black as an ink scribble[43] and so long that it reached all the way down to the ground—suffice it to say that when he walked he'd step on it with his feet. His mouth was as wide as an oven,[44] his eyes looked like two red glass lanterns lit from behind, and with his hands he'd crack a large whip made of entwined snakes and fox tails.

At the unexpected appearance of the puppeteer, everyone fell silent: no one so much as dared to breathe. You could have heard a fly buzzing. Those poor puppets, male and female alike, were shaking like so many leaves.

"Why did you come to wreak havoc in my theater?" the

puppeteer asked Pinocchio in the big, deep voice of an ogre with a bad head cold.

"Believe me, most illustrious sir, that the fault was not mine!"

"Enough of all this! This evening, we'll settle matters."

And sure enough, when the performance was over, the puppeteer went into the kitchen where he had prepared for his dinner a nice whole ram[45] that was turning slowly on a spit. And since he didn't have enough wood to finish the cooking and brown off the meat, he called Harlequin and Pulcinella and said to them:

"Bring me that puppet you'll find hanging on a nail. It seems to me he's a puppet made of very dry wood, and I'm sure that, thrown on the fire, he'll give the roast a wonderful burst of flame."

At first, Harlequin and Pulcinella hesitated, but frightened by a dirty look from their master, they did what they were told and soon returned to the kitchen, carrying poor Pinocchio. Wriggling like an eel out of water, he screamed in desperation: "Oh, Dad, Dad . . . Save me! I don't want to die, I don't want to die! . . ."

Fire-eater sneezes and forgives Pinocchio,
who then saves his friend Harlequin
from death.

The puppeteer Fire-eater (for that was his name) looked like a fearsome man—I can't say he didn't, especially with that ugly black beard of his that, like an apron, covered the whole of his chest and his legs. But deep down he wasn't a bad man. The proof is that when he saw poor Pinocchio brought before him, thrashing around in all directions and screaming "I don't want to die! I don't want to die!," he immediately began to feel moved by compassion and pity. After holding out for a good long while, in the end he couldn't stand it anymore and let rip a tremendously resounding sneeze.

At that sneeze, Harlequin, who until then had been dejected and as droopy as a weeping willow, brightened up, and a big smile appeared all over his face. Leaning down toward Pinocchio, he whispered under his breath:

"Good news, brother. The puppeteer sneezed. That's a sign he's taken pity on you. Now you're safe and sound."

Because, you see, while everyone either cries or at least pretends to dry their tears when feeling moved to pity, Fire-eater was in the habit of sneezing every time he felt tenderness for someone. It was a way like any other of letting people know how sensitive he was at heart.

After he had sneezed, the puppeteer, still acting like a grouch, shouted at Pinocchio:

"Cut out the crying! Your lamentations have given me an

unpleasant feeling here in the pit of my stomach . . . I feel a spasm that I may just . . . *Atchoo! Atchoo!*" and he sneezed again—twice.

"Bless you," said Pinocchio.

"Thank you. And are your mom and dad still alive?"[46] Fire-eater asked him.

"My dad is. My mom I never met."

"Who knows the sorrow it would cause your old father if now I threw you onto those burning coals! Poor old man! I pity him! . . . *Atchoo! Atchoo! Atchoo!*" and he sneezed again—three times.

"Bless you!" said Pinocchio.

"Thank you. On the other hand, you should pity me too, because, as you can see, I don't have any more wood to finish cooking that roasted ram, and—to tell the truth—you'd have come in very handy in this instance! But now I've been moved to compassion, and so there's nothing to be done. Instead of you, I'll put some puppet from my company to burn under the spit. Hey! Guards!"[47]

At this command, two wooden guards immediately appeared. They were very, very tall and very, very lanky, with oil lamp-shaped hats on their heads, and they were holding drawn sabers.

The puppeteer said to them in a wheezing voice:

"Go get me that Harlequin there, tie him up nice and tight, and then chuck him on the fire to burn. I want my ram well roasted!"

Just imagine poor Harlequin! So great was his fright that his knees gave way and he fell facedown on the ground.

Pinocchio, at the sight of such a heartrending scene, went to throw himself at the puppeteer's feet. Weeping inconsolably and getting the hair of Fire-eater's tremendously long beard soaked in tears, he began to say in an imploring voice:

"Have pity, Mr. Fire-eater! . . ."

"There are no misters here!" replied the puppeteer sternly.

"Have pity, Mr. Knight! . . ."

"There are no knights here!"

"Have pity, Mr. Lord! . . ."

"There are no lords here!"

"Have pity, Your Excellency! . . ."

Hearing himself called Excellency, the puppeteer immediately pursed his lips tight, and having suddenly become more humane and approachable, he said to Pinocchio:

"So then, what do you want from me?"

"I beg you to pardon poor Harlequin! . . ."

"In this case, there is no pardon to be taken into consideration. Since I spared *you*, I have to have *him* put onto the fire, because I want my ram well cooked."

"In that case," Pinocchio shouted boldly, jumping to his feet and flinging away his little hat made of bread, "in that case I know well what my duty is. Go ahead, guards! Tie me up and throw me onto those flames. It's not fair that poor Harlequin, my true friend, should die for me! . . ."

These words, uttered in a loud voice and a heroic tone, brought tears to the eyes of all the puppets present at the scene. The guards themselves, even though they were made of wood, were crying like a couple of baby lambs.

At first Fire-eater remained cold and unmoved, like a block of ice. But then, as slowly as could be, he too began to feel moved—and to sneeze. And after four or five sneezes, he opened his arms tenderly and said to Pinocchio:

"You are such a good boy! Come here and give me a kiss."

Pinocchio ran to him right away, and climbing up the puppeteer's beard like a squirrel, he went to set a beautiful kiss on the tip of his nose.

"So the pardon has been given?" asked poor Harlequin in a faint voice that you could barely hear.

"The pardon has been given!" answered Fire-eater. Then he added, sighing and shaking his head:

"Oh well! I'll settle for eating a half-raw ram tonight. But next time: whoever it is better watch out!"

At the news that the pardon had been granted, all the puppets ran onto the stage and, having turned on the lights above and below as for a gala evening, they started to jump and dance. When dawn came they were still dancing.

*The puppeteer Fire-eater gives Pinocchio five
gold coins so that he can take them to his dad,
Geppetto. Instead, Pinocchio lets the Fox and
the Cat trick him, and he goes off with them.*

The next day Fire-eater called Pinocchio aside and asked him:

"What's your father's name?"

"Geppetto."

"And what's his job?"

"Being poor."

"Does he make a lot of money doing it?"

"He earns so much as to never have a cent in his pocket. Just think that to buy my spelling book for school he had to sell the only coat he had—a coat that, what with the patches and repairs, was one big mess."

"Poor devil! I almost feel sorry for him. Here are five gold coins. Go take them straight to him and give him my best regards."

Pinocchio, as you can imagine, thanked the puppeteer a thousand times. He hugged the puppets in the company one by one—even the guards. And beside himself with joy, he set off to go back home.

But he hadn't traveled more than a quarter of a mile when along the way he met a Fox with a crippled foot and a Cat that was blind in both eyes. They were slowly walking along, helping each other, as good companions in misfortune will. The Fox, who was limping, leaned on the Cat, and the Cat, who was blind, let the Fox guide him.

"Good morning, Pinocchio," the Fox said to the puppet, greeting him politely.

"How do you know my name?" asked Pinocchio.

"I know your dad well."

"Where'd you see him?"

"I saw him on his doorstep yesterday."

"And what was he doing?"

"He was standing in his shirtsleeves and he was so cold he was shivering."

"Poor Dad! But, God willing, as of today he won't shiver anymore! . . ."

"Why is that?"

"Because I've become a fine gentleman."

"*You* a fine gentleman?" said the Fox, who started laughing in a coarse and derisive way. And the Cat too was laughing. But so as not to show it, he was combing his whiskers with his front paws.

"There's nothing funny about it," cried Pinocchio resentfully. "I'm really sorry to make your mouths water, but these here—if you know anything about this stuff—are five beautiful gold coins."

And he pulled out the coins given to him by Fire-eater.

At the pleasing sound of the coins, the Fox, with an involuntary movement, stretched the leg that seemed withered and the Cat popped his eyes wide open, so they looked like two green lanterns, but then he closed them again immediately—and indeed Pinocchio didn't notice a thing.

"So now," asked the Fox, "what are you planning on doing with those coins?"

"First of all," replied the puppet, "I want to buy my dad a beautiful new coat, all gold and silver and with buttons made of diamonds. And then I want to buy a spelling book for myself."

"For yourself?"

"That's right. Because I want to go to school and study hard."

"Look at me!" said the Fox. "Because of my silly enthusiasm for studying, I lost a leg."

"Look at me!" said the Cat. "Because of my silly enthusiasm for studying, I went blind in both eyes."

Right at that moment a white Blackbird, who was perched on the hedge along the road, gave its usual call and said:

"Pinocchio, don't pay any attention to advice from the wrong sort of friends, otherwise you'll regret it!"

Poor Blackbird, if only he had never said that! The Cat, with one great leap, pounced on him and, without giving him the time to even say "*Ouch!*," ate him up in one big bite—feathers and all.

Having eaten the bird and wiped his mouth, the Cat closed his eyes again and started acting blind as he had before.

"Poor Blackbird," said Pinocchio to the Cat. "Why were you so mean to him?"

"I did it to teach him a lesson. That way, next time, he'll know not to stick his nose into other people's conversations."

They had gotten more than halfway to Geppetto's house when the Fox, stopping all of a sudden, said to the puppet:

"Do you want to double your gold coins?"

"What do you mean?"

"How'd you like to turn your five miserable *zecchini*[48] into a hundred, a thousand, or maybe even two thousand?"

"You bet I would! And how would I do that?"

"It's very simple. Instead of going back home, you should come with us."

"And where do you want to take me?"

"To Dodoland."[49]

Pinocchio thought about it for a while, and then said resolutely:

"No, I don't want to go there. I'm almost home, and I want to get back to where my dad is: he's waiting for me. Poor old man, who knows how much he worried yesterday, not seeing me come back! Unfortunately I was a bad son, and the Talking Cricket was right when he said: 'Disobedient kids will come to no good in this world.' I've learned the hard way, because lots of terrible things have happened to me,[50] and also last night in Fire-eater's house, I ran the risk of . . . Brrr! I get goose bumps just thinking about it!"

"So," said the Fox, "you really want to go back home? Well, just go ahead then—and tough on you!"

"Tough on you!" repeated the Cat.

"Think hard about it, Pinocchio, because you're turning your back on good fortune."

"On good fortune!" repeated the Cat.

"Your five gold coins, from one day to the next, would have turned into two thousand."

"Two thousand!" repeated the Cat.

"But how on earth is it possible that they turn into so many?" asked Pinocchio, his mouth wide open in astonishment.

"I can tell you right away," said the Fox. "You see, in Dodoland there is a blessed field that everyone calls the Field of Miracles.[51] You dig a small hole in this field and you put a gold coin in it, for example. Then you cover the hole with a little bit of dirt, you water it with two buckets of water from a fountain, you chuck a good pinch of salt on it, and in the evening you go to bed without a care in the world. Meanwhile, during the night, the gold coin sprouts and blooms, and the next morning, when you arrive back in the field bright and early— what do you find? You find a beautiful tree, laden with as many gold coins as a beautiful head of wheat has grains in the month of June."

"So therefore," said Pinocchio, more and more bewildered, "if I buried my five gold coins in that field, how many would I find there the next morning?"

"It's a very easy calculation," replied the Fox. "One that you can do on the tips of your fingers.[52] Say every gold coin yields a bunch of five hundred gold coins. Multiply the five hundred by five and the next morning you'll find yourself with two thousand five hundred shiny, tinkling gold coins."

"Oh, what a wonderful thing!" shouted Pinocchio, dancing for joy. "As soon as I pick the gold coins, I'll take two thousand for myself and the other five hundred I'll give to you two as a present."

"A present for us?" shouted the Fox, taking offense and claiming to be hurt. "Good Lord, no way!"

"No way!" repeated the Cat.

"We," continued the Fox, "don't work for sordid gain. We work solely to make others rich."

"Others!" repeated the Cat.

"What good people!" Pinocchio thought to himself. And then and there, forgetting about his dad, the new coat, the spelling book, and all the good resolutions he had made, he said to the Fox and the Cat:

"Let's go immediately. I'm coming with you."

The Red Crayfish Inn

They walked on and on and on—until in the end, as evening was approaching, they arrived dead tired at the Red Crayfish Inn.[53]

"Let's stop here for a little while," said the Fox, "just to have a bite to eat and rest for a few hours. At midnight we'll set out again to be at the Field of Miracles tomorrow at dawn."

Once they were inside the inn, the three of them sat down at a table, but no one was hungry.

The poor Cat, since he had a seriously upset stomach, couldn't manage to eat more than thirty-five red mullets with tomato sauce and four portions of Parmesan tripe. And since it seemed to him that the tripe wasn't tasty enough, he asked to have extra butter and grated cheese—three times!

The Fox would have been happy to nibble on something as well, but since the doctor had prescribed a mighty strict diet for him,[54] he had to make do with a simple dish of hare in sweet and sour sauce with a very light side order of fattened young hens and little young roosters. After the hare, he had them bring him, as an appetite enhancer, a modest stew[55] of various kinds of partridge, rabbit, frogs, lizards, and sweet white raisins—after which he wanted nothing more. He was feeling so nauseated from the food, he said, that he couldn't bear to bring anything else near his mouth.

The one who ate least of all was Pinocchio. He asked for a quarter of a walnut and a tiny little crust of bread, and left everything on his plate. The poor kid, with his thoughts constantly fixed on the Field of Miracles, had gotten a case of premature gold coin indigestion.

When they had finished their dinner, the Fox said to the inn-keeper:

"Give us two good rooms, one for Mr. Pinocchio and the other for me and my companion. Before we leave again, we'll take a nap. Remember, though, that at midnight we want to be woken up in order to continue our journey."

"Yessir," answered the innkeeper, and winked at the Fox and the Cat as if to say "I get it: we understand one another! . . ."

As soon as Pinocchio got into bed he instantly fell asleep and began to dream. And in his dream he felt as if he were in the middle of a field, and the field was full of little trees laden with bunches, and the bunches were laden with gold coins that, moving in the wind, made a *ding, ding, ding* sound as if they were saying "Come and get us, whoever wants us." But when Pinocchio got to the best part of the dream—that's to say, when he reached out to grab handfuls of all those beauti-ful coins and stuff them in his pockets—he found himself sud-denly woken up by three vigorous knocks at the bedroom door.

It was the innkeeper who had come to tell him that mid-night had struck.[56]

"And are my companions ready?" the puppet asked him.

"They're a lot more than ready! They left two hours ago."

"Why on earth were they in such a hurry?"

"Because the Cat got a message that his eldest kitten, who is suffering from chilblains, is in danger of losing his life."

"And did they pay for dinner?"

"What are you talking about? Those two are too polite to go insulting a fine gentleman like you in such a way."

"A pity! That insult would have pleased me hugely!" Pinoc-chio said, scratching his head. Then he asked:

"And where did they say they would wait for me, those good friends?"

"At the Field of Miracles tomorrow morning at the break of day."

Pinocchio paid one gold coin for his own dinner and that of his companions, and then left.

But you could say that he left groping his way, because outside the inn the dark was so dark that you couldn't see from here to there. In the countryside all around you couldn't hear a leaf stir. Only some spooky night birds that, flying across the road from one hedge to another, would hit Pinocchio's nose with their wings. And jumping back in fear, he'd shout "Who's there?" and the echo in the distant hills would repeat: "Who's there? Who's there? Who's there?"

Meanwhile, as he made his way forward, he saw on the trunk of a tree a minute little animal that was translucent, with a pale and opaque glow, like a little night-light in a transparent porcelain lamp.

"Who are you?" Pinocchio asked him.

"I'm the shadow of the Talking Cricket," replied the tiny creature in a feeble little voice that seemed to come from the afterlife.

"What do you want from me?" said the puppet.

"I want to give you some advice. Go back and take the remaining four gold coins to your poor dad, who is weeping and in utter despair because he hasn't seen you."

"Tomorrow my dad is going to be a fine gentleman, because these four gold coins are going to turn into *two thousand* gold coins."

"My boy, don't trust those who promise to turn you into a rich man overnight. Usually they're either madmen or swindlers! Listen to *me*, go back."

"But *I* instead want to go on."

"The hour is late! . . ."

"I want to go on."

"The night is dark . . ."

"I want to go on."

"The way is dangerous . . ."

"I want to go on."

"Remember that kids who want to follow their every whim and do things their own way sooner or later come to regret it."

"The same old story. Good night, Cricket."

"Good night, Pinocchio, and may the heavens above save you from dew and murderers."

As soon as he had said these last words, the Talking Cricket all of a sudden went out, the way an oil lamp goes out when you blow on it, and the road was left even darker than before.

*Pinocchio, because he didn't listen to the
Talking Cricket's advice, runs into murderers.*

"Really!" the puppet said to himself starting off again. "We poor kids get such a bad deal! Everyone always getting after us. Everyone lecturing us. Everyone giving us advice. If we were to let them have their say, they'd all get it into their heads that they were our dads and our teachers—all of them, even Talking Crickets! So now, since I didn't want to listen to that bore of a Cricket, who knows how many misfortunes— according to him—I might run into! I might even run into murderers! Good thing I don't believe in murderers—nor have I ever. *I* think murderers were invented by dads just to scare kids who want to go out at night. And then, even if I *did* meet them here in the road—would they by any chance make me uncomfortable? No way. I'd put my face up to theirs and shout: 'Mr. Murderers, what do you want from me? Just you know— there's no fooling around with me! So off you go to do your own thing—and no talking back!' Faced with a lecture like that, given with an air of confidence, those poor murderers—I can just picture them—they'd flee like the wind. And if by any chance they were to be so impolite as to not want to run away—then *I'd* run away, and so it'd be over with . . ."

But Pinocchio wasn't able to finish his musings, because at that point he thought he heard behind him a very slight rustle of leaves.

He turned to look, and in the dark he saw two ghastly black figures bundled up in coal sacks, who were running after him in leaps and bounds on their tiptoes, as if they were ghosts.

"Here they are for real!" Pinocchio said to himself, and not knowing where to hide his four gold coins, he put them in his mouth—to be precise, under his tongue.

Then he tried to run away. But he hadn't even taken the first step when he felt himself grabbed by the arms and heard two terrifying, hollow voices that said to him:

"Your money or your life!"

Pinocchio, unable to answer in words because of the coins in his mouth, made a myriad of gestures and gesticulations to signal to the two hooded figures, whose eyes were all you could see through the holes in the sacks, that he was a poor puppet, and didn't have a penny in his pocket—not even a fake one!

"Come on, come on! Enough with the blabbering and out with the money!" the two bandits shouted threateningly.

And the puppet motioned with his head and his hands, as if to say: "I have none."

"Out with the money or you're dead," said the taller murderer.

"Dead!" repeated the other.

"And after we've killed you, we'll kill your dad too."

"Your dad too."

"No, no, no! Not my poor dad!" shouted Pinocchio in despair. But by shouting like that, he made the gold coins tinkle in his mouth.

"Ah! You scoundrel! So you hid the gold coins under your tongue, did you? Spit 'em out, right away!"

But Pinocchio—he stood firm.

"Ah! So you're pretending you're deaf, are you? Just you wait a minute and we'll take care of this and make you spit them out!"

Sure enough, one of them seized the puppet by the tip of his nose[57] and the other grabbed him by his chin, and there and then they started pulling him roughly, one in this direction and the other in that, so as to force him to open his mouth wide—but no way. The puppet's mouth was as if it had been nailed and riveted shut.

So the shorter murderer pulled out a terrifying knife and

tried to stick it between the puppet's lips as a lever and a chisel. But Pinocchio, as quick as lightning, clamped down on the murderer's hand with his teeth, and after he had severed it in one bite, he spat it out. And just imagine Pinocchio's astonishment when, instead of a hand, he saw a little cat's paw.

Emboldened by this first victory, he wrenched himself free of the murderers' clutches, and having jumped over the hedge that ran beside the road, he started to escape into the countryside. The murderers began to run after him, like two dogs after a hare. The one who had lost his paw was running with just one leg—and no one ever figured out how he managed that.

After running almost ten miles, Pinocchio couldn't take anymore. So, feeling he was done for, he climbed the trunk of a very tall pine tree[58] and seated himself at the very top of the branches. The murderers too tried to climb the tree, but after they got halfway up the trunk, they slipped and, as they fell back down onto the ground, skinned their hands and feet.

But they didn't let that defeat them. Instead, they gathered some dry wood to make a bundle at the foot of the tree and set it on fire. In no time at all, the pine tree started to burn and then to blaze, like a candle stirred by the wind. Pinocchio, seeing that the flames were climbing higher and higher, and not wanting to die the death of a roast pigeon, took a great leap from the top of the tree, and then off he went running again through fields and vineyards. And the murderers? Right behind him, always behind him, never tiring.

Meanwhile, the first light of day was beginning to show, and the chase was still on when all of a sudden Pinocchio found his way barred by a very deep, wide ditch, full of foul, filthy water, the color of coffee-and-milk. What to do? "One, two, three!" shouted the puppet, and giving himself a long running start he leapt to the other side. And the murderers also jumped, but not having gauged the distance well . . . *kersplash!* . . . into the ditch they fell. Pinocchio, who heard the thud and the splash, shouted as he laughed and kept on running:

"Enjoy your swim, Mr. Murderers!"

He was picturing them good and drowned when instead, turning around to have a look, he realized they were both running after him, still bundled up in their sacks, and gushing water like a couple of worn-out baskets full of holes.

The assassins run after Pinocchio, and after catching up with him, they hang him from a branch of the Big Oak.

The puppet, having lost all hope, was just at the point of throwing himself to the ground and giving up when, looking all around, he saw, in the midst of the gloomy green of the trees, something gleaming in the distance: a little house as white as snow.

"If I could draw enough breath from my lungs to reach that house, maybe I'd be saved," he said to himself.

And without further ado, he started to run full speed again through the woods.

After running in desperation for almost two hours, finally, completely out of breath, he arrived at the door of that little house and knocked.

No one answered.

He started knocking again more vigorously—because he could hear the sound of the footfalls and the breathless panting of his two pursuers.

The same silence.

Once he realized his knocking was getting him nowhere, in desperation he started to kick the door and butt it with his head. At that point, a pretty little girl looked out the window. She had blue hair,[59] and her face was as white as a waxen image. Her eyes were closed and her hands were crossed on her chest. Without moving her lips at all, she said, in a tiny, feeble voice that seemed to come from the afterworld:

"No one lives in this house. Everyone is dead."

"At least *you* could open the door for me!" shouted Pinocchio, weeping and pleading for her help.

"I'm dead too."

"Dead? Then what are you doing there at the window?"

"I'm waiting for my coffin to come take me away."

As soon as she had said these words, the little girl disappeared, and the window closed without a sound.[60]

"Oh, beautiful little girl with blue hair," Pinocchio shouted, "open the door, for heaven's sake! Have pity on a poor boy pursued by murd—"

But before he could finish the word, he felt himself being seized by the neck and heard the same two terrifying voices, which growled menacingly:

"Now you won't get away from us again!"

The puppet, seeing death flash before his eyes, started to shake so violently that you could hear the clattering of the joints in his legs and the four gold coins under his tongue.

"So?" the murderers asked him. "Are you going to open that mouth of yours—yes or no? Ah! You won't answer? . . . Don't worry, because this time *we'll* make you open it! . . ."

And pulling out two long, frightening knives as sharp as razors—*zang* . . . they stabbed him twice between the kidneys.

But the puppet—lucky for him—was made of very hard wood,[61] so the blades shattered into a thousand pieces and the murderers were left holding the knife handles and staring each other in the face.

"*I* know!" said one of them at that point. "We need to hang him! Let's hang him!"

"Let's hang him!" repeated the other.

No sooner said than done, they tied his hands behind his back and, passing a noose around his neck, they hanged him and left him to dangle from the branch of a large tree known as the Big Oak.[62]

Then they sat themselves down on the grass and waited for the puppet to give his last kick. But the puppet, after three hours, still had his eyes open, his mouth closed, and was kicking more than ever.

Finally, tired of waiting, they turned to Pinocchio and said sneeringly:

"Farewell until tomorrow. When we come back here, we hope you'll have done us the courtesy of letting us find you already nice and dead and with your mouth open."

With that, they left.

Meanwhile, a gusting north wind had gotten up. Blowing and howling with rage, it slammed the poor hanged puppet here and there, making him swing violently—like the clapper of a bell ringing in celebration. The swinging was causing him to have stabbing pains, and the noose, getting tighter and tighter around his throat, was preventing him from breathing.

Little by little his eyes grew foggy, and although he felt death approaching, still he was hoping that from one moment to the next some compassionate soul would pass by and help him. But after waiting and waiting, when he saw that no one— absolutely no one—appeared, at that point, close to death, he remembered his poor dad, and stammered:

"Oh, Dad! If only you were here! . . ."[63]

And he didn't have the breath to say more. He closed his eyes, opened his mouth, stiffened his legs, gave a big shudder, and remained there, as if completely rigid.[64,65]

*The beautiful Little Girl with blue hair has the
puppet taken down and retrieved. She puts
him to bed and calls three doctors to find
out whether he's dead or alive.*

While poor Pinocchio, having been hanged by the murderers
from a branch of the Big Oak, seemed more dead than alive,
the beautiful Little Girl[66] with blue hair looked out the window again. Moved to pity by the sight of the poor puppet who
was hanging from his neck and dancing a jig at each gust of
the north wind, she patted her hands together, clapping three
times.

Immediately after this signal, there was a great rushing
sound of wings flapping with fervent urgency. And a giant falcon came and landed on the windowsill.

"What is your command, my gracious Fairy?" asked the
Falcon, lowering his beak in a gesture of reverence. Because,
you see, the Little Girl with blue hair was, after all, none other
than a very kind fairy who had been living close to that wood
for more than a thousand years.

"Do you see that puppet dangling from a branch of the
Big Oak?"

"I do."

"Well then, fly straight down there, and with your powerful
beak cut through the knot that is keeping him suspended in
the air. Then lay him down delicately on the grass at the foot
of the Oak."

The Falcon flew away and after two minutes returned, saying:

"That which you commanded has been done."

"And how was he? Dead or alive?"

"He looked dead, but he can't yet be properly dead, because as soon as I undid the noose that had been tightened around his throat, he let out a sigh and muttered under his breath: 'Now I feel better! . . .'"

So the Fairy patted her hands together, clapping twice, and a magnificent Poodle appeared, walking upright on his hind legs, exactly as if he were a human being.

The Poodle was dressed as a coachman in fancy livery. He was wearing a little tricorn hat trimmed with gold braid, a white wig with curls that went tumbling down his neck, a chocolate-colored jacket with diamond buttons, and two large pockets for the bones that his mistress gave him at lunchtime. He had knee breeches made of crimson velvet, silk stockings, low-cut little shoes, and on his behind he had a kind of umbrella slipcover, in blue satin, to put his tail in when it started to rain.

"Be a good boy, Medoro,"[67] said the Fairy to the Poodle. "Have the most beautiful carriage in my stable prepared and take the road to the wood. When you get to the Big Oak, you'll find a poor, half-dead puppet on the grass. Pick him up gently, lay him on the cushions of the carriage just as he is, and bring him here to me. Have you understood?"

The Poodle, to show that he had understood, shook the blue satin slipcover on his behind three or four times, and set off like a racehorse.

After just a little while, a beautiful little carriage that was the color of air[68] left the stable. It was completely padded with canary feathers and lined on the inside with whipped cream and custard and ladyfingers. The little carriage was pulled by a hundred pairs of small white mice, and the Poodle,[69] sitting on the box-seat, cracked his whip to the right and left, as a coachman does when he's afraid he's late.

A quarter of an hour still hadn't gone by when the little carriage returned, and the Fairy, who was waiting at the door of the house, picked up the puppet and took him into a nice little bedroom that had mother-of-pearl walls. Then she summoned the most famous doctors in the neighborhood.

The doctors arrived immediately, one after the other: first a Crow, then an Owl and a Talking Cricket.

"I would like to know from you illustrious gentlemen," said the Fairy, turning to the three doctors gathered around Pinocchio's bed, "I would like to know from you illustrious gentlemen whether this unfortunate puppet is dead or alive."

At this invitation, the Crow, stepping forward first, felt Pinocchio's pulse; then he felt his nose, then his little toes. And when he had felt properly, he solemnly pronounced these words:

"My belief is that the puppet is well and truly dead. But if by any regrettable chance he were not dead, then that would be a sure indication that he was still alive!"

"I'm sorry," said the Owl, "to have to contradict my illustrious friend and colleague the Crow. For me instead the puppet is still alive. But if by any regrettable chance he were not alive, then that would be a sure sign that he was *truly* dead."

"What about you? Aren't you going to say anything?" the Fairy asked the Talking Cricket.

"I say that the cautious doctor—when he doesn't know what he's talking about—the best thing he can do is to keep quiet. Besides, that Puppet there . . . his face isn't new to me. I myself have known him for quite some time! . . ."

Pinocchio, who until then had been as still as a real piece of wood, had a sort of convulsive shudder that made the whole bed shake.

"That puppet there," continued the Talking Cricket, "is a consummate rascal . . ."

Pinocchio opened his eyes and then immediately closed them again.

"He's a low-down little scoundrel, a slacker, a lazy bum . . ." Pinocchio hid his face under the sheets.

"That puppet there is a disobedient son, who will make his poor dad die of a broken heart! . . ."

At that point, the sound of suppressed weeping and sobbing

could be heard in the room. Just imagine how everyone felt when, having lifted the sheets a little, they realized that the one weeping and sobbing was Pinocchio.

"When the dead cry, it means they're on the way to recovering," said the Crow solemnly.

"It pains me to contradict my illustrious friend and colleague," interjected the Owl, "but for me, when the dead cry, it's a sign they're sorry to die."

Pinocchio eats the sugar, but doesn't
want to take his medicine; though when
he sees the gravediggers coming to carry
him away, he takes it. Then he tells a lie,
and as punishment his nose grows.

As soon as the three doctors had left his room, the Fairy went to Pinocchio's side and, after putting her hand on his forehead,[70] realized that he was wracked by a raging fever.

So she dissolved a white powder[71] in half a glass of water and, handing it to the puppet, said lovingly:

"Drink it, and in a few days you'll be well."

Pinocchio looked at the glass, made a face, and then asked mournfully:

"Is it sweet or bitter?"

"It's bitter, but it'll be good for you."

"If it's bitter, I don't want it."

"Trust me. Drink it."

"Me? I don't like bitter stuff."

"Drink it, and when you've drunk it, I'll give you a sugar ball, to take away the taste."

"Where's the sugar ball?"

"Here it is," said the Fairy, bringing out a golden sugar bowl.[72]

"First I want the sugar ball, and then I'll drink that nasty bitter water . . ."

"You promise?"

"Yes . . ."

The Fairy gave him the sugar ball, and Pinocchio, after

having chewed it up and gulped it down in no time, said, licking his lips: "Wouldn't it be great if sugar too were a medicine . . . ? I'd be cleaning out my system every day."

"Now keep your promise and drink these few droplets of water that'll bring you back to health."

Pinocchio reluctantly took the glass in his hand and stuck the tip of his nose into it. Then he brought it up to his mouth. Then he went back to sticking the tip of his nose into it. Finally, he said:

"It's too bitter! Too bitter! I can't drink it."

"How can you say that if you haven't even tasted it?"

"I can imagine it! I can tell by the smell. First I want another sugar ball . . . and then I'll drink it! . . ."

So the Fairy, with all the patience of a good mom, placed another ball of sugar in his mouth; and then she presented him with the glass all over again.

"I can't drink it like this!" said the puppet, making all sorts of faces.

"Why not?"

"Because that pillow that I have down there on my feet is bugging me."

The Fairy took the pillow off his feet.

"What's the use? I can't drink it like that either."

"What else is bothering you?"

"The door to the room is bugging me, because it's half open."

The Fairy went and closed the door.

"Anyhow . . ." cried Pinocchio, bursting into tears, "this nasty bitter water . . . I don't want to drink it. No! No! No!"

"My dear boy, you're going to regret it . . ."

"I don't care . . ."

"Your illness is serious . . ."

"I don't care . . ."

"The fever will carry you off to the next world in a matter of hours . . ."

"I don't care . . ."

"You're not afraid of death?"

"Not even a little bit afraid! . . . I'd rather *die* than drink that nasty medicine."

At this point, the door of the room flew open. In came four rabbits as black as ink,[73] and on their shoulders they were carrying a little coffin.

"What do you guys want from me?" cried a terrified Pinocchio, pulling himself up in bed.

"We've come to get you," answered the biggest rabbit.

"To get me . . . ? But I'm not dead yet!"

"Not *yet*. But you have only a few minutes left to live, since you refused to drink the medicine that would have cured you of your fever . . ."

"Oh, my dear Fairy, oh my dear Fairy," the puppet then began to yell, "give me that glass right away[74] . . . Hurry, for pity's sake, because I don't want to die. No . . . I don't want to die."

And taking the glass in both hands, he emptied it in one gulp.

"Oh well," said the rabbits with an air of resignation. "This time we came for nothing." And, hoisting the little coffin back onto their shoulders, they left the room, grumbling and muttering under their breath.

The fact is that after a few minutes, Pinocchio jumped down off the bed completely recovered, because wooden puppets, you see, have the privilege of seldom falling ill and of getting well very quickly.

Seeing him running and romping around the room, all lively and cheerful like a young little rooster, the Fairy said to him:

"So my medicine really did you some good?"

"You bet! It brought me back to this world!"

"So why, then, did you have me begging you to drink it?"

"It's that we kids—we're all like that! We're more afraid of medicine than of illness."

"Shame on you! Kids should know that good medicine, taken in time, can save them from a serious illness—maybe even from dying . . ."

"Oh! But next time I won't have to be begged so much! I'll remember those black rabbits, with the coffin on their shoulders . . . and so I'll pick up the glass right away and down it'll go! . . ."

"Now, come here a moment and tell me how it was that you found yourself in the hands of those murderers."

"It went like this—Fire-eater the puppeteer gave me some gold coins and told me, 'Here you go, take them to your Dad!' and instead, on the way I ran into a Fox and a Cat, two very respectable people, who said to me, 'Would you like those few coins to become a thousand and two thousand? Come with us, and we'll take you to the Field of Miracles.' And I said, 'Let's go.' And they said, 'First let's stop here at the Red Crayfish Inn, and we'll go on after midnight.' And me—when I woke up—they weren't there anymore, because they'd already left. So I started walking at night, and the dark was so dark it seemed impossible, so that on the road I ran into two murderers inside two coal bags who said to me, 'Give over the money,' and I said, 'I don't have any,' because—the four gold coins—I'd hidden them in my mouth, and one of the murderers tried to put his hands in my mouth, and I, with one bite, bit off his hand and spat it out, but instead of a hand I spat out a little cat's paw. And the murderers were running after me, and I ran and ran till they caught up with me, and they hanged me by the neck from a tree in this wood, saying, 'Tomorrow we'll come back here and then you'll be dead and with your mouth open, so we'll take away the gold coins that you've hidden under your tongue.'"

"So now, where have you put the four gold coins?" asked the Fairy.

"I lost them!" answered Pinocchio; but that was a lie, because instead he had them in his pocket.

As soon as he had told the lie, his nose, which was already long, immediately grew longer,[75] by the width of a couple of fingers.[76]

"And where did you lose them?"

"In the wood near here."

At this second lie his nose kept growing.

"If you lost them in the wood near here," said the Fairy, "we'll look for them and we'll find them: because all that you lose in the wood here you always find again."

"Oh! Well, now that I remember correctly," replied the

puppet, getting himself all tangled up, "the four coins . . . I didn't lose them, but without realizing it I swallowed them while drinking your medicine."

At this third lie, his nose grew in such an extraordinary way that poor Pinocchio could no longer turn in any direction. If he turned this way, he bumped his nose on the bed or the windowpane; if he turned that way, he bumped it on the walls or the door of the room; if he raised his head a little more, he ran the risk of sticking it into one of the Fairy's eyes.

And the Fairy kept looking at him and laughing.

"Why are you laughing?" the puppet asked her, all confused and concerned about that nose of his that was growing so fast you could see it happening before your eyes.

"I'm laughing about the lie you told."

"How do you know I told a lie?"

"My dear boy, you can recognize lies right away, because there are two kinds: there are lies that have short legs and lies that have a long nose. Yours happens to be of the kind that has a long nose."[77]

Pinocchio, not knowing where to hide because he felt so ashamed, tried to escape from the room, but he wasn't able to. His nose had grown so long that he could no longer fit through the door.

Pinocchio runs into the Fox and the Cat again, and goes with them to plant the four gold coins in the Field of Miracles.

As you can imagine, the Fairy let the puppet cry and howl for a good half hour, because of that nose of his that wouldn't fit through the bedroom door anymore. And she did it to teach him a good lesson and to cure his bad habit of telling lies—the worst habit a kid can have. But when she saw him transformed and with his eyes bulging from his head in desperation, moved to pity, she clapped her hands. At this signal, there flew into the room about a thousand large birds called Woodpeckers. And having all landed on Pinocchio's nose, they started pecking at it so busily and incessantly that in a few minutes his enormous and unnecessarily large nose was reduced to its natural size.

"You're so good, my dear Fairy," said the puppet, drying his eyes, "and I love you very much!"

"I love you too," answered the Fairy, "and if you want to stay here with me, you can be my little brother and I will be your good sister . . ."

"I'd love to stay . . . But what about my poor dad?"

"I've worked it all out. You dad has already been told, and before night falls, he'll be here."

"Really?" cried Pinocchio, jumping for joy. "So, my dearest Fairy, if you wouldn't mind, I'd like to go meet him along the way. I can't wait to give that poor old man a big kiss. He's suffered so much because of me!"

"Go ahead, but be careful not to get lost. Take the road to the wood, and I'm sure you'll run into him."

Pinocchio left, and as soon as he entered the wood, he started to run like a little deer. But when he got to a certain point, almost facing the Big Oak, he stopped, because he thought he heard someone in the bushes. And sure enough he saw, as they were emerging onto the road—guess who?—the Fox and the Cat, which is to say the two travel companions with whom he had had dinner at the Red Crayfish Inn.

"Here's our dear Pinocchio!" shouted the Fox, hugging and kissing him. "How come you're here?"

"How come you're here?" repeated the Cat.

"It's a long story," said the puppet, "and I'll tell you about it when we have time. But—I'll tell you this—the other night, when you left me alone at the Inn, I ran into murderers along the way . . ."

"Murderers?" Oh, my poor friend! And what did they want?"

"They wanted to steal my gold coins."

"Unspeakable lowlifes! . . ." said the Fox.

"Very unspeakable lowlifes!" repeated the Cat.

"But I started to run away," the puppet continued, "but they kept close behind me, until they caught up with me and hanged me from the branch of that oak . . ."

And Pinocchio motioned toward the Big Oak, which was a stone's throw away.

"Have you ever heard anything worse than that?" said the Fox. "What a world it is that we are doomed to live in! Where will gentlefolk like us find a safe haven?"

While they were speaking in this way, Pinocchio realized that the Cat was limping with his right front leg, because he was missing his little paw—claws and all. So he asked him:

"What did you do to your paw?"

The Cat wanted to say something in reply, but he got mixed up. So the Fox jumped in.

"My friend is too modest, which is why he won't answer. I'll answer for him. You see, an hour ago, we met this old wolf on the road. He was half dead from hunger and begging for a handout.[78] Since we didn't have so much as a fishbone to give him, what did my friend do? My friend, who really has a heart of gold, bit off one of his front paws and threw it to that poor creature, so he could satisfy his hunger."

And the Fox, so saying, wiped away a tear.

Pinocchio, also moved, went up to the Cat and whispered in his ear:

"If all cats were like you, mice would be so lucky! . . ."

"And now what are you doing around here?" the Fox asked the puppet.

"I'm waiting for my dad, who should be getting here at any moment."

"And what about your gold coins?"

"I still have them in my pocket, minus one that I spent at the Red Crayfish Inn."

"And to think that, instead of four coins, they could become a thousand or two thousand tomorrow! Why don't you listen to my advice? Why don't you go plant them in the Field of Miracles?"

"Today it's impossible. I'll go there another day."

"Another day will be too late! . . ." said the Fox.

"Why?"

"Because that field has been bought by a rich gentleman, and as of tomorrow nobody will be allowed to plant money there."

"How far is the Field of Miracles from here?"

"Just over a mile. Do you want to come with us? In half an hour you'll be there. You plant the four coins right away. After a few minutes, you harvest two thousand, and this evening you'll be back here with your pockets full. Do you want to come with us?"

Pinocchio hesitated a little before answering, because he thought of the good Fairy again. And of old Geppetto. And of the warnings of the Talking Cricket. But then he ended up doing what all kids with no good sense and no heart do. He ended up, that is, flicking his head a little and saying to the Fox and the Cat:

"Let's go, then. I'm coming with you."

And they left.

After walking half a day, they arrived in a city called Catch-dupesburg.[79] As soon as he entered the city, Pinocchio saw that all the streets were full of mangy dogs who were yawning with hunger, sheep who had been shorn and were shaking from the cold, hens without their crests and wattles who were begging for a corn kernel, large butterflies who could no longer fly because they had sold their beautiful, colorful wings, peacocks with no tails who were ashamed to show themselves, and pheasants who were quietly wandering around, mourning the loss of their shimmering golden and silver feathers that were by then gone forever.

Through this crowd of bums and shamefaced paupers, from time to time there passed a lordly carriage, bearing some Fox or Magpie or some fearsome bird of prey.[80]

"And where is the Field of Miracles?" Pinocchio asked.

"It's here—a stone's throw away."

No sooner said than done, they crossed the city and exited the walls, stopping in a solitary field that looked more or less like any other field.

"Here we are," said the Fox to the puppet. "Now get down on the ground and dig a little hole in the field with your hands and put the gold coins in it."

Pinocchio did as he was told. He dug the hole, put in his four remaining gold coins, and then covered the hole with some dirt.

"Now, then, go to the ditch that's nearby, get a bucketful of water, and water the ground where you planted the coins."

Pinocchio went to the ditch, and since he didn't have a bucket just then and there, he took off one of his old shoes, filled it with water, and poured the water over the soil that was covering the hole. Then he asked:

"Is there anything else to do?"

"Nothing else," replied the Fox. "Now we can leave. Then you come back in about twenty minutes and you'll find a little shrub already growing out of the ground, its branches laden with gold coins.

The poor puppet, beside himself with joy, thanked the Fox

and the Cat a thousand times and promised them a wonderful present.

"We don't want presents," answered those two fiends. "For us, it's enough to have taught you how to get rich without having to sweat—we're as happy as can be."

That said, they bid farewell to Pinocchio, and having wished him a plentiful harvest, they went about their own business.

Pinocchio is robbed of his gold coins, and as
punishment, he gets four months in jail.

The puppet went back to the city and began counting the minutes one by one, and when it seemed to him it might be time—immediately he took the road again to go back to the Field of Miracles.

While he was walking along hurriedly, his heart was pounding hard and going *tick-tock, tick-tock* like a hall clock when it's going really fast. And in the meantime he was thinking to himself:

"What if instead of one thousand gold coins, I found two thousand on the branches of the tree? . . . Or if instead of two thousand, I found five thousand? Or if instead of five thousand I found one hundred thousand? Oh, what a swell gentleman I'd become then! . . . I'd like to have a beautiful mansion, a thousand little wooden horses and a thousand stables to play with, a cellar stacked with rosolio[81] and alkermes,[82] and a library full of candied fruit, cakes, panettones, crunchy nougat bars, and big wafer sticks smothered in whipped cream.

Pipe-dreaming this way, he got close to the field and stopped to see if maybe he could catch sight of any trees that had branches laden with coins. But he didn't see a thing. He went on another hundred paces—but not a thing. He went into the field . . . He went right to the little hole where he had buried his gold coins—and not a thing. At that point he became pensive and, forgetting the rules of the Guide to Good Manners[83] and those of social graces, pulled a hand out of his pocket and with the tips of his fingers gave his head a good long scratch.

Just then he heard a burst of laughter that rang in his ears, and, turning around, he saw a large Parrot in a tree who was grooming the few feathers he had left.

"What's so funny?" Pinocchio asked him in a peevish voice.

"I'm laughing because, while I was grooming my feathers, I tickled myself under my wings."

The puppet didn't answer. He went to the ditch and, after filling the same old shoe with water, started to pour it over the soil that covered the gold coins.

And at that point, another burst of laughter, even more insolent than the first, made itself heard in the lonely silence of the field.

"Now listen!" shouted Pinocchio, getting angry. "Are you going to tell me what you're laughing about, you ill-mannered Parrot?"

"I'm laughing about the dodoes[84] who believe all the nonsense they're told and who let themselves be ensnared by those more cunning than they are."

"Are you perhaps speaking about me?"

"Yes, I'm speaking about you, poor Pinocchio—you who are so witless[85] you believe that you can plant and harvest money in a field the way you plant beans and pumpkins. I thought so too once, and I still bear the scars today. Today—alas, too late!—I've had to accept that to make some money honestly you have to know how to earn it with either the toil of your own hands or the ingenuity of your own brain."

"I don't get it," said the puppet, who was already starting to shake in fear.

"Okay, then! I'll spell it out," the Parrot went on. "You see, while you were in the city, the Fox and the Cat came back here to the field; they took the gold coins you'd buried, and then they fled like the wind. And good luck catching up with them now!"

Pinocchio's mouth fell open. Not wanting to believe the Parrot's words, he started to use his hands and nails to dig the earth he had watered. And he dug, and dug, and dug until he had made such a deep hole that you could have fit a haystack into it upright. But the gold coins were no longer there.

Seized by despair, he ran all the way back to the city and went straight to the courthouse, to report the two crooks who had robbed him to the judge.

The judge was a big ape of the Gorilla species: a big, old ape, respected because of his honorable age, his white beard, and particularly his gold-rimmed glasses, which had no lenses and which he was forced to wear at all times because of an eye inflammation that had been tormenting him for years.

Pinocchio, standing before the judge, recounted in every last detail the story of the iniquitous fraud of which he had been the victim. He gave the first names, the last names, and a description of the crooks, and ended by asking for justice to be done.

The judge was very kindly disposed to what he heard. He became sincerely engaged with the story: he was touched, he was moved, and when the puppet had nothing more to say, he reached for a bell and rang it.

At once, at the sound of the bell, two mastiffs in guards' uniforms made their appearance.

The judge, gesturing toward Pinocchio, said to the guards:

"This poor devil has been robbed of four gold coins. Therefore seize him and put him straight in jail."

The puppet, upon being hit out of the blue with this sentence, was dumbfounded and wanted to protest. But the guards, so as not to get lost in unnecessary time-wasting, covered his mouth and led him off to the cooler.

There he had to stay for four months—four very long months. And he would've stayed even longer if it hadn't been for a very fortunate turn of events. Because, you see, the young Emperor who reigned over Catchdupesburg, having won a great victory over his enemies, ordered lavish public celebrations, ornamental illuminations, firework displays, horse and bicycle races. And as a sign of yet further jubilation, he also ordered the jails to be opened and for all the crooks to be set free.

"If the others are leaving prison, I want to be set free too," Pinocchio said to the jailer.

"No, not you," replied the jailer, "because you're not part of the contingent."

"I beg your pardon," answered Pinocchio, "but I'm a crook too."

"In that case, you're absolutely in the right," said the jailer. And removing his hat respectfully, and bidding him farewell, he opened the doors of the prison and let him run off.

Freed from jail, Pinocchio heads back home to the Fairy, but along the way he runs into a terrible snake and is caught in a claw trap.

You can just imagine how happy Pinocchio felt to be free. Without hanging around to quibble, he immediately left the city and retook the road that should have led him back to the Fairy's little house.

Since it was raining, the road had become a morass and you could sink into it up to your knees. But the puppet gave it no thought. Consumed by excitement because he was going to see his dad and his dear, blue-haired sister, the puppet ran in leaps and bounds like a greyhound. As he ran, the mud splattered higher than his little hat. Meanwhile, he was saying to himself:

"What a lot of misfortunes have befallen me . . . And I deserve them! Because I'm a stubborn and obstinate puppet . . . and I always want to do things my way, without paying attention to all those who care for me and have a thousand times more sense than I do! . . . But from now on, I want to make a resolution to change my life and become a well-behaved and obedient boy . . . In any case, I've already understood that if kids are disobedient, they always end up getting a bad deal and never get things right. But I wonder if my dad waited for me? . . . Will I find him at the Fairy's house? I haven't seen him, poor man, in such a long time that I'm dying to smother him in kisses and cuddle him to death. And will the Fairy forgive me for my bad behavior? . . . And to think of all the attention and loving care that she lavished on me . . . To think that if I'm still alive today, I owe it to her! . . . Does a more ungrateful and heartless boy than me even exist? . . ."

As he was talking to himself like this, all of a sudden he stopped in fright and took four steps back.

"What had he seen?"[86]

He had seen a large Snake, stretched out across the road. It had green skin, eyes of fire, and a pointed tail that was pouring out smoke like a chimney.

You cannot imagine how scared the puppet was. He went back about a quarter of a mile and sat down on a little pile of stones, waiting for the Snake to clear out and go about his own business once and for all, leaving the roadway free.

He waited an hour. Two hours. Three hours. But the Snake was still there, and even from a distance you could see his fiery eyes shining red and the column of smoke coming out from the tip of his tail.

So, telling himself he had the courage, Pinocchio got close. When he was just a few paces away, with a sweet, small, wheedling voice, he said to the Snake:

"Excuse me, Mr. Snake, might you do me the favor of moving a bit to one side, so as to let me pass?"

It would have been the same if he had spoken to a brick wall. No one moved.

So he resumed in the same little voice:

"You see, Mr. Snake, I'm going home, where my dad is waiting for me, and I haven't seen him in a very long time! . . . Would you mind, therefore, if I continued on my way?"

He waited for a sign in reply to his question, but it never came. Instead, the Snake, who until then had been perky and full of life, became very still and almost rigid. His eyes closed and his tail stopped smoking.

"Could he really be dead?" said Pinocchio, rubbing his hands together in delight. And not wasting a second, he got ready to climb over the Snake and continue along the road. But he hadn't even finished lifting his leg when the Snake reared up suddenly, like a spring that had been released, and the puppet, bounding back in fear, tripped and fell to the ground.

In fact he fell so badly that he ended up with his head stuck in the mud and his legs up in the air.

At the sight of the puppet, head down and thrashing his legs back and forth at an incredible speed, the Snake was seized by such a fit of laughter that he laughed and laughed and laughed, and in the end, because of the strain of laughing too much, a blood vessel in his chest burst open—and this time he really did die.

So Pinocchio started running again in order to get to the Fairy's house before dark. But along the way, since he could no longer stand the terrible pangs of his hunger, he jumped into a field with the idea of picking a few bunches of muscatel grapes. If only he hadn't!

As soon as he got to the foot of the vine, *crack* . . . he felt his legs seized by two sharp pieces of metal that made him see all the stars in the sky.

The poor puppet had been caught in a claw trap, set by farmers to catch the large weasels who were the scourge of all the chicken coops in the neighborhood.

*Pinocchio is caught by a farmer who forces
him to be the watchdog for a chicken coop.*

Pinocchio, as you may well imagine, started to weep and yell
and beg for help. But his tears and his cries were useless, because there was not a house in sight, and not a soul passed by
on the road.

Meanwhile, night fell.

A little because of the pain from the trap that was cutting
into his shins, and a little because of the fear of being alone in
the dark in the middle of those fields, the puppet began to feel
as if he were going to faint—when all of a sudden, seeing a
firefly[87] pass over his head, he called out to her and said:

"Dear little Firefly, would you be so kind as to free me from
this agony? . . ."

"You poor kid!" replied the firefly, stopping to look at him
sympathetically. "How did you get your legs caught up in
those sharp pieces of metal?"

"I came into the field to pick a couple of bunches of these
muscatel grapes, and . . ."

"But were the grapes yours?"

"No . . ."

"So who taught you to take stuff that belongs to other
people?"

"I was hungry . . ."

"Hunger, my dear boy, is not a good reason to walk off with
stuff that doesn't belong to us . . ."[88]

"It's true! It's true!" shouted Pinocchio, weeping. "But next
time I won't do it again."

At this point their conversation was interrupted by the faint noise of approaching footsteps. It was the owner of the field, who was tiptoeing over to see if any of the weasels, who had been eating his chickens during the night, had been caught by the bite of the trap.

And upon pulling a lantern out from under his cape, he was astonished when he realized that—instead of a weasel—a boy had been trapped.

"Ah! You little thief!" said the enraged farmer. "So it's you who takes my chickens?"

"It's not me, it's not me!" shouted Pinocchio, sobbing. "I came into the field just to take a couple bunches of grapes! . . ."

"Anyone who steals grapes is perfectly capable of stealing chickens too. Leave it to me: I'll teach you a lesson that you'll not forget in a long time."

And after opening the trap, he seized the puppet by the scruff of the neck and carried him home, holding him the way you would carry a suckling lamb.

Once he reached the farmyard in front of the house, he hurled him to the ground and, keeping a foot on his neck, said:

"It's late now, and I want to go to bed. We'll settle matters tomorrow. Meanwhile, since the dog that kept guard at night died today, you will immediately take his place. You will be my watchdog."

No sooner said than done, he forced a large collar covered in brass spikes over Pinocchio's neck, and tightened it in such a way that the puppet couldn't take it off by slipping it over his head. A long metal chain was fastened to the collar, and the chain was attached to the wall.[89]

"If it starts to rain tonight," said the farmer, "you can go curl up in that little wooden shed. Inside it there's still the straw that my poor old dog used as a bed for four years. And if by some stroke of bad luck any burglars come, remember to keep your ears pricked—and to bark."

After this final admonition, the farmer went into the house, bolting the door shut. Poor Pinocchio was left crouched in the farmyard, more dead than alive from the cold and from his hunger and fear. And every so often, angrily jabbing his hands between his neck and the collar that was squeezing his throat, he'd say as he wept:

"It serves me right! . . . Unfortunately, it serves me right! I insisted on being a slacker, a loafer . . . I insisted on listening to the advice of the wrong sort of friends, and because of this, fate keeps tormenting me. If I'd been a good little kid, like so many; if I'd felt like studying and working; if I'd stayed home with my poor dad, I wouldn't be here now, in the middle of the fields, being the watchdog of a farmer's house. Oh! If only I could be born again! . . . But now it's too late, and I must bear my lot with patience!"

Having vented his despair with this outburst that really and truly came from his heart, he made his way inside the little shed and fell asleep.

Pinocchio discovers the thieves, and,
as a reward for his loyalty, he is set free.

Pinocchio had been sleeping deliciously well for more than two hours when around midnight he was woken up by the sound of whispering and a buzzing murmur of funny little voices he thought he heard in the farmyard. He stuck his nose out of the doorway of the shed and saw four small, dark-furred creatures gathered in a huddle. They looked like cats. But they weren't cats: they were weasels, little carnivorous animals, and very gluttonous, especially when it came to eggs and young hens. Breaking away from the others, one of the weasels approached the doorway of the shed and whispered:

"Good evening, Melampus."[90]

"My name isn't Melampus," replied the puppet.

"Oh, so who *are* you?"

"I'm Pinocchio."

"And what are you doing in there?"

"I'm being a watchdog."

"Oh, so where's Melampus? Where is the old dog who lived in this little shed?"

"He died this morning."

"Died? Poor thing! He was so kind! . . . But judging by the way you look—you too seem like an amiable dog."

"I beg your pardon! I'm *not* a dog! . . ."

"Oh, so what are you?"

"I'm a puppet."

"And you're being a watchdog?"

"Regrettably, I am. It's my punishment! . . ."

"Well then, I'll propose to you the same deal that I had with the late Melampus. And you'll like it."

"And what might this deal be?"

"We'll come over to visit the chicken coop once a week, as we've done in the past, and we'll take away eight hens. We'll eat seven of them and give you one, on condition—obviously—that you pretend you're asleep and that it never even occurs to you to bark and wake up the farmer."

"And is that really what Melampus did?"

"He did. And we all got along well. Always. So sleep peacefully, and be assured that, before we go, we'll leave you a ready plucked hen on your shed for tomorrow's breakfast. Have we understood each other?"

"Only too well! . . ." answered Pinocchio. And he tilted his head a few times in a somewhat threatening way, as if to say: "We'll be talking about this again soon!"

When the four weasels thought they had the situation under control, they went straight to the chicken coop, which in fact was very close to the dog's shed. And with their teeth and little claws, they went furiously at the wooden door that kept the small entrance shut, until they managed to breach it. Then, they slipped in one after another. But they had barely all gotten in when they heard the small door slam shut again with great violence.

It was Pinocchio who had closed it, and, not satisfied with just having closed it, to be even surer he put a large stone in front of it to keep it propped shut.

And then he started to bark. Barking just like a watchdog, he went *"Bow-wow, bow-wow."*

Upon hearing the barking, the farmer leapt out of bed, grabbed his shotgun, looked out the window,[91] and asked:

"What's going on?"

"Burglars!" replied Pinocchio.

"Where are they?"

"In the chicken coop."

"I'll be right down."

And sure enough, in no time at all the farmer came down

and ran into the chicken coop. After catching the weasels and securing them inside a sack, he said to them with true glee:

"So you finally fell into my hands! I could punish you, but I'm not that mean! Instead, I'll be satisfied with taking you to the innkeeper of the neighboring town, who'll skin you and cook you in a sweet-and-sour sauce, like hares. It's an honor you don't deserve, but generous men like me don't bother with such trivial details! . . ."

Then he went over to Pinocchio. Petting him lavishly, he asked him, among other things:

"How did you manage to uncover the scheme of these four little thieves? And to think that Melampus, my faithful Melampus, never realized anything! . . ."

At that point, the puppet could have said what he knew. That is, he could have told the farmer about the shameful deal between the dog and the weasels. But remembering that the dog was dead, he immediately thought to himself:

"What's the use of accusing the dead? . . . The dead are dead, and the best thing that can be done is to let them be! . . ."

"When the weasels arrived in the farmyard, were you awake or asleep?" the farmer went on to ask him.

"I was asleep," answered Pinocchio. "But the weasels woke me up with their chitter-chatter, and one even came over here to the little shed to say to me, 'If you promise not to bark and wake up the owner, we'll give you a nice little ready-plucked hen! . . .' You understand, huh? Just think! Having the nerve to propose such a deal to *me*! Because I want you to know that I'm a puppet that—well, I may have all the faults in the world, but I'll never be an accomplice of dishonest people!"

"Good boy!" cried out the farmer, slapping him on the back. "Those feelings do you credit. And to prove how satisfied I am with you, I'll set you free to go back home, starting right now."

And he took the dog collar off Pinocchio.

Pinocchio mourns the death of the beautiful
Little Girl with blue hair. Then he meets
a Pigeon who brings him to the seashore,
where Pinocchio throws himself into the
water to go help his dad, Geppetto.

As soon as Pinocchio no longer felt the oppressive, humiliating weight of that collar around his neck, he started to flee through the fields and didn't stop for a single moment until he reached the main road that should have led him back to the Fairy's house.

Once he had reached the main road, he turned around to look down onto the plain below and with the naked eye could see perfectly the wood in which he had had the misfortune to meet the Fox and the Cat. Amid all the trees, he could make out the top of the Big Oak from which he had been hanged, dangling by his neck. But he looked here and looked there, yet he couldn't see the house of the beautiful blue-haired Little Girl.[92]

At that moment he had a kind of sad presentiment and began running with all the strength he had left in his legs. After a few minutes he reached the meadow where the little white house once stood. But the little white house[93] was no longer there. Instead, there was a small marble stone on which could be read in capital letters these painful words:

HERE LIES
THE BLUE-HAIRED LITTLE GIRL
WHO DIED OF GRIEF
FOR HAVING BEEN ABANDONED BY HER
LITTLE BROTHER PINOCCHIO

The state in which the puppet was left, after he had more or less made out these words—well, I leave it to you to imagine. He fell facedown on the ground, and, smothering the mortuary marble in kisses, he burst into a flood of tears. He wept all night, and the next morning around dawn he was still weeping, although his eyes had no more tears left. And his cries and laments were so piercing and heart-wrenching that all the hills around kept repeating their echo.[94]

In between sobs, he said:

"Oh, my dear Fairy, why did you die? . . . Why did *I* not die instead of you—I who am so bad while you were so good? . . . And my dad—where could he be? Oh, my dear Fairy, tell me where I can find him, because I want to be with him forever, and never leave him again. Never, never, never . . . ! Oh, my dear Fairy, tell me it's not true that you're dead! . . . If you really love me . . . if you love your little brother, come back to life[95] . . . be alive again as you were before! . . . Doesn't it hurt you to see me alone and abandoned by everyone? . . . If the murderers come, they'll hang me from the branch of the tree all over again . . . and then I'll die forever. What do you want me to do here, alone in this world? Now that I've lost you and my dad, who will feed me? Where will I sleep at night? Who will make me my new little jacket? Oh! It'd be better, a hundred times better, if I died too! Yes, I want to die! . . . *Boo-hoo-hoo! . . .*"

And while he was in such a fit of desperation, he made as if to tear his hair out, but since his hair was made of wood, he couldn't even have the satisfaction of sticking his fingers in it.

Meanwhile, there passed by, up in the air, a large Pigeon[96] who, having stopped with his wings outstretched, asked Pinocchio from a great height:

"Tell me, little boy, what are you doing down there?"

"Can't you see? I'm crying!" said Pinocchio, raising his head toward the voice and wiping his eyes with the sleeve of his little jacket.

"Tell me," continued the Pigeon. "Do you, by any chance, know a puppet among your friends whose name is Pinocchio?"

"Pinocchio? . . . Did you say Pinocchio?" repeated the puppet, immediately jumping to his feet. "*I*'m Pinocchio!"

The instant he heard this reply, the Pigeon swooped down and fluttered to the ground. He was larger than a turkey.

"So you must also know Geppetto?" he asked the puppet.

"Do I *know* him? He's my poor dad! Maybe he spoke to you about me? But is he still alive? Answer me, for pity's sake:[97] is he still alive?"

"I left him three days ago at the seashore, on the beach."

"What was he doing?"

"He was making himself a little boat with his own hands in order to cross the Ocean. It's been more than four months that that poor man has been going all over the world looking for you. And since he was never able to find you, now he has gotten it into his head to go looking for you in the distant lands of the New World.[98]

"How far is the beach from here?" Pinocchio asked with breathless anxiety.

"More than five hundred miles."[99]

"Five hundred miles? Oh, my dear Pigeon, wouldn't it be wonderful if I had your wings! . . ."

"If you want to go there, I'll take you."

"How?"

"By having you ride on my back. Are you very heavy?"

"Heavy? On the contrary! I'm as light as a leaf."

So then and there, without another word, Pinocchio jumped onto the Pigeon's back and, putting one leg on this side and the other on that, the way horse riders do, he shouted, as happy as can be: "Giddyap, giddyap, little horsey, 'cause I really want to get there soon! . . ."

The Pigeon flew up into the air, and after a few minutes he was soaring so high he could almost touch the clouds. Having reached that extraordinary height, the puppet became curious to look down and was seized by such fear and dizziness that, to avoid the danger of tumbling off, he wrapped his arms around the neck of his feathered mount, clinging to him as tightly as a vine to its stake.

They flew all day long. Toward evening, the Pigeon said:

"I'm really thirsty!"

"And I'm really hungry!" added Pinocchio.

"Let's stop at that dovecote for a few minutes, and then we'll start our journey again so we can be at the seashore, on the beach, tomorrow morning at dawn."

They went inside the empty dovecote, where there was just a basin full of water and a small basket heaped with vetch peas.

The puppet had never, in the whole of his life, been able to stand vetch peas: going by what he said, they made him nauseated and turned his stomach. But that evening he ate enough to burst his belly, and when he had almost finished them, he turned to the Pigeon and said:

"I'd never have thought vetch peas were so good!"

"My boy," replied the Pigeon, "you need to bear in mind that when hunger really speaks up for itself and there's nothing else left to eat, even vetch peas[100] become delicious! Hunger is neither picky nor greedy!"

After rapidly eating their little snack, they resumed their journey, and off they went! The next morning they arrived at the beach on the seashore.

The Pigeon set Pinocchio on the ground, and shying away from the inconvenience of hearing himself thanked for his good deed, he took to the air again and disappeared.

The beach was filled with people who were shouting and gesticulating as they looked out to sea.

"What's happened?" Pinocchio asked a little old lady.

"What's happened is that a poor dad, having lost his child, insisted on getting into a tiny boat to go look for him on the other side of the sea. But the sea's very rough today, and the tiny boat is about to go down . . ."

"Where *is* the tiny boat?"

"There it is—over there: straight along the line of my

finger," said the old woman, pointing to a small boat that, seen from that distance, looked like a nutshell with a teeny-weeny little man inside it.

Pinocchio sharpened his focus in that direction, and having looked very carefully, he let out a piercing scream:

"That's my dad! That's my dad!"

Meanwhile, the tiny boat, battered around by the fury of the waves, kept disappearing among the combers, only to re-surface again. Pinocchio was standing on the tips of his toes on the top of a tall rock, and he wouldn't stop calling his dad's name and signaling wildly with his hands and his handker-chief and even the little hat that he wore on his head.

It seemed as if Geppetto, even though he was a long way from the beach, had recognized his son, because he also took off his hat and waved and, by gesticulating furiously, made the puppet understand that he would have gladly returned to the beach, but the sea was so swollen it wouldn't let him use his oars to get closer to land.

All of a sudden, a terrible wave came—and the boat disap-peared. They waited for the boat to resurface . . . But it was not to be seen again.

"Poor man," said the fishermen who were gathered on the beach. And grumbling[101] a prayer under their breath, they turned to go back to their homes.

It was then that they heard a scream of desperation, and looking back, they saw a little kid who, from the top of a rock, threw himself into the sea, shouting:

"I want to save my poor dad!"

Pinocchio, being made entirely of wood, floated easily and swam like a fish. One moment you could see him disappear underwater, dragged by the power of the swell, the next he would reappear out of the water with a leg or an arm, far out to sea. In the end, they lost sight of him and could see him no longer.

"Poor boy!" said the fishermen who were gathered on the beach. And grumbling a prayer under their breath, they turned to go back to their homes.

Pinocchio gets to the island of the Busy Bees
and finds the Fairy again.

Driven by the hope of reaching his poor dad in time to help him, Pinocchio swam all night long.

And what a horrible night it was! Rain came down in torrents. It hailed. It thundered fearsomely and with such lightning that it seemed like daytime.

At first light he could make out, not very far away, a long strip of land. It was an island in the middle of the sea.

So he tried everything he could to get to the beach—but it did him no good. The waves, chasing one another and each crashing into the next, were tossing him around as if he were a twig or a bit of straw. In the end, and fortunately for Pinocchio, there came a wave so powerful and so overwhelming that it hurled him onto the sand along the shore.

Such was the force of the impact when he hit the ground that all his ribs and all his joints clattered. But he immediately consoled himself by saying:

"Once again, I've had a narrow escape!"

Meanwhile, the sky cleared up little by little, the sun came out in all its splendor, and the sea turned as calm as could be and as smooth as silk.

So the puppet hung his clothes out in the sun to dry and started looking this way and that, in case by any chance he could see, on that immense expanse of water, a tiny boat with a little man inside. But after having looked carefully, he could see nothing but sky, sea, and the odd sail of a ship—but so far away that it looked as small as a fly.

"If only I knew the name of this island," he kept saying. "If only I knew if this island were inhabited by well-mannered people, I mean people that don't have the habit of hanging kids from tree branches . . . But who can I ask? Who, if no one is around?"

This idea of finding himself alone—all alone, truly alone—in the middle of that big uninhabited land made him feel so melancholy that he was just on the point of crying when all of a sudden there passed, not far from the shore, a large fish that was peacefully minding its own business, with its head out of the water.

Not knowing what name to call him by, the puppet shouted out to him in a loud voice to make himself heard:

"Hey, Mr. Fish, would you allow me to have a word?"

"Even two," answered the fish, who was a dolphin, and so courteous that just a few like him can be found in all the seas of the world.

"Would you be so kind as to tell me if there are any towns on this island where one can get something to eat without the danger of being eaten?"

"There are for sure," replied the Dolphin. "Actually, you'll find one not far from here."

"And which way do I go to get there?"

"You have to take that lane down there, on the left, and keep walking. Just follow your nose. You can't go wrong."

"Tell me something else. Since you wander the sea all day and night, you wouldn't by any chance have come across a tiny boat with my dad in it?"

"And who is your dad?"

"He's the best dad in the world, just as I'm the worst son that could ever be."

"With the storm there was last night," the Dolphin replied, "the tiny boat will surely have gone under."

"And what about my dad?"

"By now he's likely been swallowed by the terrible shark that in the past few days has been spreading carnage and devastation in our waters."

"Is this shark really very big?" asked Pinocchio, who was already starting to tremble in fear.

"Is it *big*? . . ." replied the Dolphin. "Just so you get the idea, let me tell you that it's larger than a five-story building and its awful mouth is so wide and deep that a railroad train could easily pass through it with its engine going."

"Oh, my goodness!"[102] cried the puppet in fear. And having got dressed again with the utmost haste, he turned to the Dolphin and said to him:

"See you again, Mr. Fish. Forgive me for troubling you and thank you so much for your kindness."

That said, he immediately set off down the lane and started to walk fast—so fast that it almost seemed like he was running. And at every small noise he heard, he'd turn around briskly to look back, for fear of seeing himself chased by that terrible shark as big as a five-story house and with a railroad train in its mouth.

After half an hour on the road he got to a small town called Busybeesville.[103] The streets were swarming with people who were running here and there on their errands: everyone was working, everyone had something to do. You couldn't find an idler or a lazy bum no matter how hard you looked.

"I see," said that slacker Pinocchio. "This town is not for me! I was not born to work!"

Meanwhile, hunger was tormenting him, because by then he hadn't eaten anything for twenty-four hours—not even a dish of vetch peas.

What to do?

He had only two ways to satisfy his hunger: either to ask to do some work, or to beg for a coin or a morsel of bread.

Begging made him feel ashamed, because his dad had always lectured him on the fact that only the elderly and the infirm have the right to beg. The true poor in this world, deserving of assistance and compassion, are only those who, because of age or illness, find themselves condemned to a life in which they can no longer manage to make a living with the sweat of their own brow. All the others have a duty to work. And if they don't work and go hungry—so much the worse for them.

Meanwhile, down the road there came a man who was

drenched in sweat and out of breath. He was single-handedly pulling, and with the greatest effort, two carts piled with coal.

Pinocchio thought he looked like a good man, judging by his face, so he went up to him and, casting his eyes down in shame, said to him in a whisper:

"Could you spare me a *soldo*, because I feel like I'm starving to death?"

"Not just one *soldo*," replied the coalman. "I'll give you *four*, on one condition: that you help me pull these two carts of coal to my house."

"I'm shocked!" replied the puppet, almost insulted. "For your information, I have never worked as a donkey: I have never pulled a cart! . . ."

"So much the better for you!" The coalman said. "Well then, my boy, if you really feel like you're starving to death, eat two nice slices of your pride and be careful you don't get indigestion."

After a few minutes, a bricklayer came down the street, carrying a basket of mortar on his back.

"Kind sir, could you spare a *soldo* for a poor boy who's yawning from hunger?"

"Gladly. Come with me and carry the mortar," answered the bricklayer. "And instead of one *soldo*, I'll give you five."

"But mortar is heavy," retorted Pinocchio, "and I don't want to work hard."

"If you don't want to work hard, my boy, then have fun yawning, and much good may it do you."

In less than half an hour, twenty more people came past. Pinocchio begged from them all, but they all answered:

"Aren't you ashamed of yourself? Instead of being a good-for-nothing on the streets, go look for some work and learn to make a living!"

Finally, there came along a good little woman carrying two jugs of water.

"Would it be all right, good woman, if I took a drink of water from your jug?" Pinocchio asked—he had a burning thirst.

"Feel free to drink, my boy!" said the woman, setting the two jugs on the ground.

When Pinocchio had drunk like a sponge, he muttered under his breath, wiping his mouth:

"So, I've gotten rid of my thirst. If only I could get rid of my hunger the same way! . . ."

The good little woman, on hearing these words, immediately said:

"If you help me carry one of these jugs home, I'll give you a nice piece of bread."

Pinocchio looked at the jug and said neither "Yes" nor "No."

"And with the bread I'll give you a nice dish of cauliflower in oil and vinegar," added the good woman.

Pinocchio gave the jug another look and said neither "Yes" nor "No."

"And after the cauliflower I'll give you a nice sweet filled with rosolio." [104]

At the seductive thought of this last delicacy, Pinocchio could no longer resist, and with his mind made up, he said:

"Oh well! I guess I'll carry the jug home for you."

The jug was very heavy and, not having the strength to carry it with his hands, the puppet resigned himself to carrying it on his head.

Once they had reached home, the good little lady sat Pinocchio down at a small table that had been set and laid out before him the bread, the cauliflower, and the sweet.

Pinocchio didn't eat—he gorged himself. His stomach was like an apartment that had stood empty and uninhabited for five months. [105]

Once his fierce hunger pangs had been appeased little by little, he looked up to thank his benefactress, but he hadn't finished staring at her face when he let out a long and protracted *ohhhhh . . . !* of bewilderment and sat there as if under a spell—his eyes wide open, his fork in the air, and his mouth full of bread and cauliflower.

"What ever is all this bewilderment about?" said the good woman, laughing.

"It's . . ." answered Pinocchio, stammering, "it's . . . well, it's . . . that to me you look like . . . you remind me of . . . yes, yes, yes—the same voice . . . the same eyes . . . the same

hair . . . yes, yes, yes . . . you too have blue hair . . . like her! . . .
Oh my Fairy! . . . Oh my Fairy! . . . Tell me it's you—really
you! . . . Don't make me cry anymore! If only you knew! . . . I
cried so much, I suffered so much! . . ."

And as he said this, Pinocchio was crying a flood of tears.
Dropping to the ground and kneeling, he threw his arms
around the mysterious little woman's knees.

Pinocchio promises the Fairy to behave
and study, because he is sick of being
a puppet and wants to become a good boy.

At first, the good little lady began by saying that she wasn't the little Fairy with blue hair. But then, seeing that she had been found out and not wanting to drag out the comedy any longer, she ended up by letting herself be recognized, and said to Pinocchio:

"You rascally little puppet! How did you figure out it was me?"

"It was my great love for you that told me."

"Do you remember? You left me a child and now you find me a woman—so much a woman that I could almost be your mother."[106]

"That's really wonderful for me, because this way, instead of my sister, I'll call you my mom. It's been so long that I've been dying to have a mom, just like all the other kids have! . . . But how did you manage to grow up so quickly?"

"It's a secret."

"Teach me: I'd like to grow up a little bit too. Don't you see? I've always been knee-high to a grasshopper."

"But you can't grow up," replied the Fairy.

"Why not?"

"Because puppets never grow up. They're born as puppets, they live as puppets, and they die as puppets."[107]

"Oh, I'm sick of always being a puppet!"[108] cried Pinocchio, cuffing himself on the head. "It's about time I too became a man . . ."[109]

"And you will, if you deserve it . . ."

"Really? And what can I do to deserve it?"

"Very easy. Just get used to being a good little kid."

"Well, isn't that just what I am?"

"Anything but! Good kids are always obedient—and you, instead . . ."

"And I *never* obey."

"Good kids learn to love studying and working—and you . . ."

"And, *I*, instead, am a good-for-nothing and a lazy bum all year round."

"Good kids always tell the truth . . ."

"And *I* always tell lies."

"Good kids are happy to go to school . . ."

"And school makes *me* feel sick to my stomach. But starting today I want to change my life."

"Do you promise?"

"I do. I want to become a good little kid and I want to be a comfort to my dad . . . Where could my poor dad be?"

"I don't know."

"Will I ever be lucky enough to see him and hug him again?"

"I think so. Actually I'm sure you will."

Hearing this reply, Pinocchio was so overjoyed he took the Fairy's hands and started to kiss them with such vehemence that he seemed almost beside himself. Then, lifting his head and looking at the Fairy lovingly, he asked:

"Tell me, Mommy: so it's not true that you're dead?"

"It would seem not," replied the Fairy with a smile.

"If only you knew how much pain I felt and how my throat clenched up when I read: *Here lies . . .*"

"I know. And that's why I've forgiven you. The sincerity of your suffering made me realize that you have a good heart. And good-hearted kids, even if they're a little mischievous and spoiled, always give you hope—hope, I mean, that they'll get back onto the right path. That's why I came all the way here to look for you. I'll be your mom . . ."

"Oh! What a wonderful thing!" shouted Pinocchio, jumping for joy.

"You will obey me and always do what *I* tell you."

"Gladly! Gladly! Gladly!"

"Starting tomorrow," added the Fairy, "you will begin by going to school."

Pinocchio immediately became a little less cheerful.

"Then, you'll choose a trade or a profession of your liking..."

Pinocchio became serious.

"What are you grumbling about between clenched teeth?" asked the Fairy a little resentfully.

"I was saying..." whimpered the puppet under his breath, "that by now it seems a little late to be going to school..."

"Not at all. Bear in mind that it's never too late to get an education and learn a trade."

"But I don't want to have a trade or a profession..."

"Why not?"

"Because work seems like a lot of effort to me."

"My boy," said the Fairy, "those who say that always end up either in prison or in a poorhouse. For your information, people in this world, whether born rich or poor, must do something, be busy—must work. Bad things will happen to those who let themselves fall prey to idleness. Idleness is a terrible sickness, and it must be cured immediately, from the time we are children. Otherwise, when we grow up, we become incurable."

These words touched Pinocchio's soul: he looked up, full of life, and said to the Fairy:

"I'll study, I'll work, I'll do everything you tell me to, because—well, I've gotten tired of the life of a puppet, and I want to become a boy at all costs. You promised me. Right?"

"I promised you, and now it depends on you."

*Pinocchio goes to the seashore with his
schoolmates to see the terrible Shark.*

The next day Pinocchio went to the local school.[110]

Just imagine those little rascals when they saw a puppet coming into their school! The laughter that burst out just wouldn't die down. One kid would prank him here, another there; one would snatch his hat right out of his hands, another would tug the back of his jacket; one would try to draw a big mustache under his nose,[111] another would even try to tie strings to his hands and feet to make him dance.

For a while Pinocchio was unperturbed and let things slide. But eventually he lost his patience. Turning to those who, more than the others, had teased and tormented him like horseflies, he said firmly:

"Watch out, guys: I haven't come here to be your buffoon. I respect others, and I want to be respected."

"Way to go, you idiot! You talk like a printed book!" shouted those little scoundrels, bursting with laughter. And one of them, cockier than the others, reached out to grab hold of the puppet by the tip of his nose.

But he wasn't quick enough, because Pinocchio had stretched out his leg under the table and delivered him a nice kick on the shin.

"Ouch! What hard feet!" yelled the boy, rubbing the bruise the puppet had given him.

"And what elbows! . . . even harder than his feet!" said another who, in return for his rough pranks, had gotten Pinocchio's elbow in his stomach.

The fact is that after that kick and that jab, the puppet immediately earned the respect and affection of all the schoolkids. They fussed over him and really loved him wholeheartedly.

The teacher too praised him, because he saw that Pinocchio was attentive, studious, and smart—always the first to arrive and always the last to get to his feet when school was over.

His only fault was that he mixed with too many of his schoolmates: among them were several little scoundrels well known for their reluctance to study and do themselves proud.

The teacher warned him every day. And the good Fairy too never failed to tell him and to repeat over and over again:

"Be careful, Pinocchio! Sooner or later those awful schoolmates of yours are going to make you lose your love of studying and—who knows?—maybe even cause you to bring some terrible calamity upon yourself."

"There's no danger of that!!" the puppet would reply, shrugging and touching his forehead with his finger as if to say: "There's lots of good sense in here!"

Now, what happened is that one fine day, while he was walking to school, Pinocchio ran into a gang of those same schoolmates, who went up to him and said:

"Have you heard the big news?"

"No."

"In the sea near here, a shark has turned up that's as large as a mountain."

"Really? . . . I wonder if it could be the same shark I saw when my poor dad drowned?"

"Well, *we're* going to the beach to see him. Do you want to come too?"

"Me? No, I want to go to school."

"What do you care about school? We'll go to school tomorrow. One lesson more or one less, we'll still be the same old donkeys."[112]

"And what will the teacher say?"

"Let the teacher say whatever he likes. That's what they pay him for: to grumble every day."

"And what about my mom? . . ."

"Moms never know anything," said those little fiends.

"You know what I'll do?" Pinocchio said. "I want to see the shark for reasons of my own . . . but I'll go see it after school."

"You poor dope!" shot back one of the gang. "What do you think? That a fish that size is going to stick around to please *you*? As soon as he gets bored, he's going to go straight to some other place—and that'll be that."

"How long does it take to get from here to the beach?" asked the puppet.

"In an hour we'll have gone there and back."

"So off we go! And whoever runs the fastest is the best!" shouted Pinocchio.

The starting signal having thus been given, that gang of little scoundrels started to run through the fields with their textbooks and exercise books under their arms, and Pinocchio was always ahead of everyone. It seemed as if he had wings on his feet.

From time to time, he would turn back to make fun of his friends who were a pretty long way behind, and seeing them panting and out of breath, covered in dust and with their tongues hanging out, he would laugh wholeheartedly. At that moment the luckless wretch had no idea what terrors and horrible misfortunes he was running toward! . . .

*A great big fight between Pinocchio and
his schoolmates. And because one of
them gets injured, Pinocchio is arrested
by the Carabinieri.*

As soon as he got to the beach, Pinocchio cast a long look across the sea. But he saw no shark. The sea was totally smooth, like a vast mirror.

"So where's the shark?" he asked, turning to his schoolmates.

"He might have gone to have breakfast," one of them answered, laughing.

"Or he might have flopped onto his bed to have a nap," added another, laughing even harder.

From these senseless replies and their stupid, coarse laughter, Pinocchio realized his schoolmates had played a nasty prank on him, by getting him to believe something that wasn't true. And taking it badly, he said to them in a peevish voice:

"So what now? What fun have you gotten out of making me believe that stupid little story about the Shark?"

"The fun is there for sure! . . ." shouted those little scoundrels all together.

"And what would that be? . . ."

"Making you miss school and come with us. Aren't you ashamed? Being so scrupulous and diligent every day in class? Aren't you ashamed of studying so much the way you always do?"

"What do you guys care if I study?"

"We care very much, because you make us look bad in front of the teacher . . ."

"Why?"

"Because students who study always cast a bad light on those like us who don't feel like studying. And we don't want to be made to look bad! We too have our pride! . . ."

"And so what should I do to make you happy?"

"You too should be sick of school, lessons, and the teacher—our three great enemies."

"And what if I want to keep on studying?"

"We won't have anything more to do with you, and the first chance we have, we'll get even with you! . . ."

"The truth is you almost make me laugh," said the puppet, shaking his head a little.

"Hey, Pinocchio!" shouted the biggest of the kids, going straight up to the puppet and putting his face in his. "Who do you think you are, acting like a hotshot? Don't come around here acting so cocky! . . . 'Cause if you're not afraid of us, we're not afraid of you! Remember, there's one of you, and there's seven of us."

"Seven. Like the Seven Deadly Sins," said Pinocchio, bursting out laughing.

"Did you guys hear that? He insulted all of us! He called us Deadly Sins! . . ."

"Pinocchio, say you're sorry for insulting us . . . If not, you'll regret it! . . ."

"*Cuc-koo!*" went the puppet, tapping the tip of his nose with his index finger, to make fun of them.

"Pinocchio! This is going to end badly! . . ."

"Cuc-koo!"

"You're going to get a beating like a donkey! . . ."

"Cuc-koo!"

"You're going to go back home with a broken nose! . . ."

"Cuc-koo!"

"Now *I'll* give you cuckoo!" shouted the boldest of those little scoundrels. "Meanwhile, take this as a down payment and keep it for tonight's dinner."

And saying this, he slammed a punch into Pinocchio's head.

But it was blow for blow, as they say, because the puppet, as could have been expected, immediately responded with a punch of his own. And so, from one moment to the next, the fight turned into a raging and unrelenting free-for-all.

Pinocchio, although all on his own, defended himself heroically. He made such good use of those hard wooden feet of his that he was able to keep his enemies at a respectful distance. Wherever his feet managed to land, they would always leave a bruise as a souvenir.

The kids, frustrated not to be able to tussle with the puppet hand to hand, had the bright idea of resorting to missiles. They undid the bundles in which their schoolbooks had been packed and began hurling the books at Pinocchio—the spelling books, the grammar books, *Giannettino*, *Minuzzolo*, Thouar's *Tales*, Baccini's *Baby Chick*, and other school texts.[113] But the puppet, who had a quick eye and sharp reflexes, always ducked in time, so the books, passing over his head, all landed in the sea.

Just imagine the fish! The fish, who thought all those books were stuff to eat, swarmed to the surface, but after nibbling on a page here and a frontispiece there, they would spit them straight out again, twisting their mouths as if to say, "This stuff is not for us: *we're* used to eating much better!"

The battle was getting more and more ferocious when along came a large crab that had made its way out of the water and very, very slowly crawled up onto the beach. In an ugly voice like a trombone with a cold, he shouted:

"Cut it out, you little delinquents— 'cause that's all you are! This sort of brawling between kids seldom ends well. Something unfortunate always happens! . . ."

Poor crab! He might as well have been preaching to the wind. Turning around to give him a dirty look, that rascal Pinocchio said to him rudely:

"Shut up, you irksome crab! You'd do better to suck on a couple of lichen lozenges to get rid of that sore throat. Just go to bed and try to sweat it out! . . ."

At that point the kids, who had finished throwing all their books, caught sight of Pinocchio's bundle of textbooks, which was just close by, and quickly grabbed hold of it.

Among the books was a volume bound in stiff cardboard, its spine and edges in sheepskin. It was the *Treatise on Arithmetic*. I'll leave you to imagine how heavy it was!

One of the little scoundrels got his hands on it and, taking aim at Pinocchio's head, flung it with all the strength he had in his arm. But instead of hitting the puppet, he got one of their schoolmates on the head. The boy went as white as a washed dishcloth, and said no more than these few words:

"Oh my goodness![114] Help me . . . I'm dying! . . ."

Then he collapsed flat out onto the sandy beach.

Terrified by the sight of that dead little body, the boys ran away as fast as they could, scattering in all directions. After a few minutes, they were nowhere to be seen.

But Pinocchio stayed. And even though he too felt more dead than alive from pain and fear, he ran to wet his handkerchief in the sea and started to dab his poor schoolmate's temple. All the while he was crying, and in a fit of despair he called his schoolmate by his name and said:

"Eugene! . . . my poor Eugene! . . . Open your eyes and look at me! . . . Why aren't you answering me? It wasn't me, you know, who hurt you so bad! Believe me, it wasn't me! . . . Open your eyes, Eugene . . . If you keep your eyes shut, you'll make *me* die too . . . Oh my God! How will I go back home now? . . . How will I find the courage to show my face to my good mom? What will become of me? . . . Where will I run to? . . . Where will I hide? . . . Oh! It would've been so much better, a thousand times better, if I'd gone to school! . . . Why did I listen to those schoolmates of mine? They are my downfall! . . . And the teacher had warned me! . . . And my mom had repeated it to me: beware of bad schoolmates! But I'm stubborn . . . Obstinate. And bad . . . I let everyone have their say, and then I always do things my own way! And then I have to pay for it . . . And so, ever since I've been in this world, I've not had a quarter of an hour's peace. My God! What will become of me? What will become of me? What will become of me? . . ."

Pinocchio kept on weeping, howling, punching himself in

the head, and calling poor Eugene by his name—when all of a sudden he heard a muffled sound of footsteps approaching.

He turned around: it was two Carabinieri.

"What are you doing, lying there on the ground?" they asked Pinocchio.

"I'm helping this schoolmate of mine."

"Is he sick?"

"It seems so! . . ."

"This is no sickness!" said one of the Carabinieri, bending down and looking at Eugene up close. "This boy has a wound on his temple. Who injured him?"

"Not me," stammered the puppet, who had no breath left in his body.

"If it wasn't you, then who did?"

"Not me," repeated Pinocchio.

"And what was he injured with?"

"With this book," said the puppet, picking up the *Treatise on Arithmetic*, bound in cardboard and sheepskin, to show the Carabiniere.

"And who does this book belong to?"

"It belongs to me."

"That's it: we don't need anything more. Stand right up and come with us."

"But I . . ."

"Come with us! . . ."

"But I'm innocent . . ."

"Come with us!"

Before they left, the Carabinieri called to some fishermen who at that very moment happened to be passing close to the beach in their boat, and said to them:

"We're leaving this kid in your charge. He's suffered a head injury. Carry him home and look after him. Tomorrow we'll be back to see him."

So they turned to Pinocchio and, after having put him between them, gave him orders in a soldierly tone:

"Forward march! And on the double! Otherwise you'll be sorry!"

Without the Carabinieri having to repeat themselves, the puppet started walking along the lane that led to the town. But the poor little devil didn't even really know what world he was in anymore. He felt like he was dreaming—and what a bad dream! He was beside himself. His eyes were seeing everything double, his legs were shaking, his tongue had gotten stuck to the roof of his mouth, and he could no longer utter a single word. Yet in the midst of his stupefaction and befuddlement, a needle-like thorn was piercing his heart: the thought of having to pass under the windows of his good Fairy's home between the two Carabinieri. He would rather have died.

They had already arrived and were about to enter the town when an unruly gust of wind tore Pinocchio's hat off his head and carried it about ten paces away.

"Would it be okay," the puppet asked the Carabinieri, "if I went to retrieve my hat?"

"Go ahead, but make it quick."

The puppet went, picked up the hat . . . but, instead of putting it on his head, he put it between his teeth, and then started running like mad toward the seashore. He went as fast as a bullet fired from a rifle.

The Carabinieri, who figured it would be hard to catch up with him, sent after him a large mastiff that had won first prize in all the dog races. Pinocchio ran, but the dog was faster, and everyone started looking out their windows and gathering in crowds in the street, eager to see the end of this ferocious contest.[115] But they weren't able to satisfy their curiosity, because the mastiff and Pinocchio kicked up so much dust along the road that after a few minutes nothing more of them could be seen.

*Pinocchio runs the risk of being
pan-fried like a fish.*

During that desperate race there was a terrible moment—a moment in which Pinocchio thought all was lost. Because, you see, Alidoro[116]—for that was the mastiff's name—had almost caught up with the puppet by running like crazy.

Suffice it to say that the puppet could hear the heavy breathing of that terrible beast right behind him, just a few inches away, and could even feel the waves of heat from his panting.

Luckily, by that time, the beach was close by, and you could see the sea just a few paces away.

As soon as he was on the beach, the puppet made a beautiful leap, as a frog might have done, and plunged straight into the water. Alidoro wanted instead to stop, but, carried forward by the sheer force of his running, he too ended up in the water. And the poor wretch didn't know how to swim, so he immediately started to thrash around with his paws to stay afloat. But the more he thrashed around, the more his head went under the water.

When he finally got his head back out of the water, the poor dog's eyes were wide open in terror, and he was barking:

"I'm drowning! I'm drowning!"

"Die!" Pinocchio replied to him from afar, feeling safe from any danger.

"Help me, my dear Pinocchio! . . . Save me from dying! . . ."

At those heartrending cries, the puppet, who all in all had a very good heart, was moved to compassion and, turning around toward the dog, said to him:

"But if I help you, do you promise not to give me any more trouble and not to run after me?"

"I promise! I promise! Hurry, for pity's sake, because if you hesitate another thirty seconds, I'll be dead."

Pinocchio wavered a little, but then, remembering what his dad had told him many times, that by doing a good deed you never go wrong, he swam toward Alidoro and, seizing him by the tail with both hands, brought him safe and sound onto the dry sand of the shore.

The poor dog could no longer stand up. Without intending to, he had drunk so much salt water that he was as bloated as a balloon. Even so, the puppet, not wanting to be too trusting, thought it would be prudent to dive back into the sea. As he swam away from the beach, he shouted to his rescued friend:

"Farewell, Alidoro, have a good trip back and give my best to everyone at home!"

"Farewell, Pinocchio," replied the dog. "A thousand thanks for having saved me from death. You sure did me a favor, and in this world what is given is paid back. If we get the chance, we'll speak again."

Pinocchio kept on swimming, always keeping close to land. At last, it seemed to him that he had reached a safe place. He took a look at the shore and saw a sort of cave in the rocks, from which trailed a very long strand of smoke.

"There must be a fire in that cave," he said to himself. "Good! I'll go dry myself and get warm, and then? . . . Then whatever will be, will be."

Having made up his mind, he got close to the rocks, but when he was on the point of climbing up, he felt something under the water that came up, and up, and up—and lifted him into the air. He immediately tried to escape. But it was too late because, to his astonishment, he found himself trapped in a large net in the midst of a teeming multitude of fish of every size and shape, flapping their tails and thrashing around like so many souls in despair.

At that very moment he saw, coming out of the cave, a fisherman who was so ugly—but really *so* ugly—that he looked like a sea monster. Instead of hair, he had a very thick bush of green grass on his head. The skin of his body was green; green were his eyes; green was his thick beard, and so long that it reached down to here. He looked like a giant lizard standing upright on its hind legs.

When the fisherman had pulled the net out of the sea, he shouted gleefully:

"Blessed providence! Today too I'll be able to eat my fill of fish!"

"Good thing I'm not a fish!" Pinocchio said to himself, feeling a little courage seep back into his soul.

The net, full of fish, was taken into the cave—a cave that was dark and full of smoke. In the middle, oil was frying in a great big pan and producing a smell of snuffed-out candles that was enough to take your breath away.

"Now let's see here what fish we've caught!" said the green fisherman. And with that, he plunged a giant hand into the net—a hand so big it looked like a baker's shovel—and pulled out a handful of red mullet.

"What tasty red mullet!" he said, looking at them and sniffing them with satisfaction. And after sniffing them, he tossed them into an earthenware pot with no water in it.

He repeated this several times. As he was pulling out all the other fish, he could feel his mouth watering, and he said, gloating:

"What tasty hake!

"What exquisite striped mullet!

"What delicious sole!

"What flavorsome weever fish!

"What cute anchovies, with their heads still on!"

As you may imagine, the hake, the striped mullet, the sole, the weever fish, and the anchovies all went helter-skelter into the earthenware pot, to keep the red mullet company.

The last one left in the net was Pinocchio.

As soon as the fisherman pulled him out, his great big green eyes popped out in astonishment and he shouted, almost in fright:

"What kind of fish is this? I don't remember ever having eaten a fish that looked like this!"

And he went back to looking at Pinocchio very carefully. After having looked him over meticulously from every possible angle, he finally said:

"I get it: this must be a deep-sea crab."

Pinocchio, mortified at hearing himself mistaken for a deep-sea crab, said resentfully:

"What do you mean a crab? I'm no crab. Watch how you treat me! For your information, I'm a puppet."

"A puppet?" replied the fisherman. "To tell the truth, a puppet-fish is a new one to me! So much the better! I'll eat you with even greater relish."

"*Eat* me? Don't you get it? I'm not a fish! Can't you hear that I speak and reason just like you?"

"That's a very good point," said the fisherman, "and since I see you are a fish, and that you have the good fortune to speak and reason like me—well, I'll treat you with due respect."

"And how would you do that . . . ?"

"As a token of particular friendship and esteem, I'll give *you* the choice of how you want to be cooked. Would you like to be pan-fried, or do you prefer to be cooked in a skillet with tomato sauce?"

"To tell the truth," answered Pinocchio, "if I must choose, I'd prefer instead to be set free, so I can go back home."

"You're joking! You really think I want to miss out on the opportunity to taste such a rare fish? Catching a puppet-fish in these waters is not something that happens every day. Let me take care of this: I'll fry you in a pan along with all the other fish and, just you see, you'll be happy with that. To be fried in company is always a consolation."

Poor Pinocchio, getting the drift, started to weep, and scream, and beg. And as he wept, he kept saying: "How much better it would have been if I'd gone to school! . . . I insisted on listening to my schoolmates, and now I'm paying for it! *Boohoo-hoo!* . . ."

And since he was squirming like an eel and making incredible efforts to wriggle out of the green fisherman's clutches, the fisherman took a good strong strip of reed, tied Pinocchio's hands and feet so he looked like a salami wrapped in string, and threw him into the earthenware pot along with all the others.

Then he pulled out a battered wooden platter full of flour and started to flour all the fish. And as he floured them he would throw them into the frying pan.

The first ones to dance in the oil were the poor hake, then it was the turn of the weever fish, then of the sole and the anchovies—and then came Pinocchio's time. Seeing himself so close to death (and what an awful death!), he was seized by such a fit of shaking and terror that he didn't even have the voice or the breath to plead.

The poor kid was pleading with his eyes! But the green fisherman, without even paying attention to him, rolled him around in the flour five or six times, flouring him so thoroughly from head to toe that he looked like he was made of plaster.

Then the green fisherman took Pinocchio by the head, and . . .

*Pinocchio returns to the Fairy's house. She
promises him that the next day he will no
longer be a puppet, but will become a boy.
Grand breakfast with coffee-and-milk to
celebrate this great event.*

When the fisherman was just about to throw Pinocchio into the frying pan, into the cave came a large dog that had been lured by the pungent, tasty smell of the fried fish.

"Get out of here!" the fisherman yelled menacingly at the dog, still holding the floured puppet in his hand.

But the poor dog was as hungry as four dogs put together. Whimpering and flailing his tail around, he seemed to be saying:

"Give me a mouthful of fried fish and I'll leave you alone."

"Get out of here, I said!" the fisherman repeated as he extended his leg to give the dog a kick.

But the dog, who wasn't in the habit of being pushed around when he was truly hungry, turned on the fisherman, snarling and showing him his terrible fangs.

At that moment a feeble little voice was heard in the cave, saying:

"Save me, Alidoro! If you don't save me, I'll end up fried! . . ."[117]

The dog instantly recognized Pinocchio's voice and realized, to his great astonishment, that the little voice had come from that floured bundle the fisherman was holding.

So what does he do? With one great leap, he snatches the floured bundle with his mouth and, holding it delicately in his teeth, he dashes out of the cave, and then away he goes, as quick as a flash.

The fisherman, furious at seeing the fish snatched from his hand—he had been so looking forward to eating it!—tried to run after the dog. But after a few steps he had a coughing fit and had to turn back.

Meanwhile, Alidoro, having found the lane that led back to the town, stopped and carefully put his friend Pinocchio on the ground.

"How will I ever thank you enough!" said the puppet.

"There's no need," replied the dog. "You saved me, and you reap what you sow. It's a known fact: in this world we all have to help one another."

"But how did you wind up in that cave?"

"I was still lying on the beach, more dead than alive, when the wind brought a delightful smell of fried fish from far away. That delightful smell whetted my appetite, and I followed it. Just imagine if I had gotten there a minute later! . . ."

"Don't even say it!!" shouted Pinocchio, who was still shaking with fear. "Don't even say it! If you'd gotten there a minute later, by now I'd be good and fried, eaten, and digested. *Brrr!* . . . It gives me the shivers just to think of it!"

Alidoro, laughing, held out his right paw to the puppet, who shook it vigorously as a sign of great friendship, and then they parted.

The dog headed back home, and Pinocchio, left on his own, went to a little shack not far from there, and asked a little old man who was at the door warming himself in the sun:

"Tell me, kind sir, do you know anything about a poor boy who was injured in the head and whose name was Eugene? . . ."

"The boy was brought to this shack by some fishermen, and now—"

"Now he must be dead! . . ." interrupted the grief-stricken Pinocchio.

"No—now he's *alive*! And he's already gone back home."

"Really? Really?" cried the puppet, jumping for joy. "So the wound wasn't serious? . . ."

"But it could have been serious—even deadly," replied the

little old man, "because a large hardcover book was thrown at his head."

"And who threw it at him?"

"A schoolmate of his, someone called Pinocchio . . ."

"And who is this Pinocchio?" the puppet asked, playing dumb.

"They say he's a bad kid, a lazy bum, a real troublemaker."

"Slander! It's all slander!"

"Do you know this Pinocchio?"

"By sight!" replied the puppet.

"And what do *you* think about him?"

"To me he seems like a really good kid—eager to study, obedient, devoted to his dad and his family . . ."

While the puppet was telling these barefaced lies one after another, he touched his nose and realized that it had grown more than a palm's length. So, seized with fear, he began to shout:

"Kind sir, don't pay any attention to what I've told you about him, because I know Pinocchio very well and I too can assure you that he's a bad kid—he's disobedient and a slacker, and instead of going to school he goes off, causing trouble with his schoolmates!"

As soon as he had uttered these words, his nose retracted and went back to its normal size, the way it was before.

"And why are you all white like that?" the little old man suddenly asked him.

"I'll explain . . . without noticing, I rubbed against a wall that had just been whitewashed,"[118] replied the puppet, ashamed that he had been floured like a fish, in order to be pan-fried.

"So, what did you do with your jacket, your pants, and your hat?"

"I ran into thieves and they stripped me.[119] Tell me, my good old man, you wouldn't by chance have just anything I could wear so I can go back home?"

"My boy, as far as clothes go, all I have is a little sack in which I keep lupini beans. If you want it, take it: it's over there."

Pinocchio didn't need to be told twice: he immediately took the bag of lupini beans, which was empty, and after cutting a little hole in the bottom and two holes in the sides with a pair of scissors, he slipped it on as if it were a shirt. Barely clothed in that way, he headed for town.[120]

But along the way, he didn't feel at all relaxed. He was so uneasy that he would take one step forward and one step back and, having an entire conversation with himself, said:

"How will I be able to show my face to my good Fairy? What will she say when she sees me? . . . Will she be willing to forgive this second escapade? . . . I bet she won't forgive me! . . . Oh! For sure she won't forgive me . . . And it serves me right: because I'm a scoundrel—I always promise to change, and then I never keep my word! . . ."

The night was already pitch dark when Pinocchio reached town, and since the weather was terrible and rain was coming down by the bucketful, he went straight to the Fairy's house with his mind made up to knock on the door and have it opened for him.

But when he got there, he felt his courage drain away, and instead of knocking he backed away about twenty paces at a run. Then he went back to the door a second time, but it came to nothing. Then he approached a third time—but nothing. The fourth time, shaking, he took the metal knocker in his hand and gave a tiny little knock.

He waited and waited, and finally, after half an hour, a window on the top floor (the house had four stories)[121] opened up, and Pinocchio saw a big snail look out. She had a little lamplight on her head, and she said:

"Who is it at this time?"

"Is the Fairy home?" asked the puppet.

"The Fairy is sleeping and doesn't want to be woken. But who are you?"

"It's me!"

"Me who?"

"Pinocchio."

"Pinocchio who?"

"The puppet, the one who lives at home with the Fairy."

"Oh! I see," said the Snail. "Wait for me there. I'll come down right away and open the door for you."

"Hurry up, for pity's sake, because I'm dying of the cold."

"My boy, I'm a snail, and snails are never in a hurry."

So an hour went by, then two—and the door still didn't open. So Pinocchio, who was shivering from the cold and the rain and the fear that was in him, plucked up all his courage and knocked a second time—and knocked louder.

At this second knock, a window opened on the floor below, and the same snail looked out.

"My lovely Snail," Pinocchio shouted up from the street, "I've been waiting for two hours! And two hours, on a terrible night like this, becomes longer than two years. Hurry up, for pity's sake!"

"My boy," that creature, who was all amiability and composure, replied from the window, "my boy, I am a snail, and snails are never in a hurry."

And the window shut again.

After a little while, it struck midnight. Then one, then two in the morning—and the door was still shut.

So Pinocchio, having lost his patience, grabbed the door knocker angrily to let fly a knock that would shake the whole building—but the knocker, which was made of metal, suddenly became a live eel that slipped through his hands and disappeared into a rivulet that was running down the middle of the street.

"Oh yeah?" cried Pinocchio, more and more blinded by rage. "If the knocker's disappeared, I'll keep on pounding on the door with my feet."

And having pulled back a little, he let fly a tremendous kick at the front door. The blow was so powerful that his foot went halfway into the wood, and when he tried to pull it out again, all his efforts proved in vain because his foot was jammed inside the door, like a riveted nail.

Just imagine poor Pinocchio! He had to spend the rest of the night with one foot on the ground and the other in the air.

Come the morning, around dawn, the door finally opened. It had taken the Snail, that good creature, a mere nine hours to come down from the fourth floor all the way to the front door. And, my goodness, had she worked up a sweat!

"What are you doing with that foot of yours stuck in the door?" she asked the puppet, laughing.

"It was a mishap.[122] See if you can free me from this torture, my lovely Snail."

"My boy, for that we need a carpenter, and I've never been a carpenter."

"Beg the Fairy on my behalf! . . ."

"The Fairy is sleeping and doesn't want to be woken."

"But what do you want me to do nailed to this door all day?"

"Have fun counting the ants that pass by in the street."

"At least bring me something to eat, because I'm feeling faint."

"Right away!" said the Snail.

In fact, after three and a half hours Pinocchio saw her return with a silver tray on her head. On the tray there was a loaf of bread, a roast chicken, and four ripe apricots.

"Here's the lunch the Fairy sends you," said the Snail.

Seeing those heavenly delights, the puppet felt thoroughly consoled. But what a disappointment he felt when he began to eat and realized that the bread was made of plaster, the chicken of cardboard, and the four apricots of realistically colored alabaster.

He wanted to cry. He wanted to give himself up to desperation. He wanted to throw away the tray and what was on it. But, instead, maybe because his sorrow was great, or maybe because of the void in his stomach—the fact is that he collapsed in a faint.

When he came to, he found himself lying on a sofa, and the Fairy was next to him.

"This time too, I forgive you," the Fairy said. "But you'll be in trouble if you play another one of your tricks on me! . . ."

Pinocchio promised and swore that he would study and that he would always behave. And he kept his word for the whole rest of the year. In fact, in the end-of-school exams, he was honored as the best student in the school, and his conduct in general was judged to be so praiseworthy and satisfactory that the Fairy, as happy as could be, told him:

"Tomorrow your wish will finally come true!"

"And what's that?"

"Tomorrow you will cease to be a wooden puppet and become a good little boy."

Those who didn't see Pinocchio's joy at this greatly longed-for news will never be able to imagine it. All his friends and schoolmates were to be invited the next day for a grand breakfast at the Fairy's house to celebrate the great event. The Fairy had two hundred cups of coffee-and-milk[123] prepared, and four hundred buns with both halves buttered. The day promised to be truly wonderful and truly joyous, but . . .

Unfortunately, in the lives of puppets there is always a "but" that ruins everything . . .[124]

Instead of turning into a boy,
Pinocchio secretly leaves for Playland
with his friend Lampwick.

As might be expected, Pinocchio immediately asked the Fairy for permission to go around the town to invite his guests, and the Fairy said to him:

"Go ahead and invite your schoolmates to tomorrow's breakfast. But remember to be back home before night falls. Is that clear?"

"I promise I'll be back home in an hour," replied the puppet.

"Be careful, Pinocchio! Kids are quick to promise, but most of the time they are slow to keep their word."

"But I'm not like the others. Me? When I say something, I stick to my word."

"We'll see. If by chance you were to disobey, it would be all the worse for you."

"Why?"

"Because kids who don't listen to the advice given to them by those who know more than they do always head straight into some kind of misfortune."

"And I sure have found that out!" said Pinocchio. "But I'm not going to fall into the same trap again!"

"We'll see if you're telling the truth."

Without another word, the puppet said goodbye to his good Fairy, who was like a mom to him, and left through the front door singing and dancing.

In little more than an hour, all his friends had been invited. Some accepted right away and good-naturedly. Others, at first, had Pinocchio insist a little, but when they were told that the buns to dip into the coffee-and-milk were going to be buttered[125] on both halves, they all ended up saying: "We'll come too—to please you."

Now, you see, of all his friends and schoolmates, there was one who was Pinocchio's favorite. His name was Romeo, but everybody called him by his nickname, Lampwick, because of his slim, trim figure—skinny and lanky—just like the new wick in a little night lamp.

Lampwick was the laziest, most mischievous kid in the whole school, but Pinocchio really cared for him. In fact, he went directly to Lampwick's house to invite him to the breakfast, but he couldn't find him. He went back a second time, but Lampwick still wasn't there. He went back a third time, but again he went in vain.

Where to track him down? Pinocchio looked for him here and looked for him there, and in the end he saw him hidden under the portico of a farmhouse.

"What are you doing there?" Pinocchio asked him as he approached.

"I'm waiting to leave . . ."

"Where are you going?"

"Far, far away!"

"And to think that I've come looking for you at home three times! . . ."

"What did you want with me?"

"You don't know about the big event? You don't know about the good fortune that's come my way?"

"What's that?"

"Tomorrow I'll be done with being a puppet and I'll become a boy like you—and like all the others."

"Much good may it do you!"

"So tomorrow, I'll be expecting you at my house for breakfast."

"But I've just told you—I'm leaving tonight!"

"When exactly?"

"In a bit."

"And where are you going?"

"I'm going to live in a country . . . that's the most wonderful country on earth: a true land of milk and honey! . . ."

"And what's it called?"

"It's called 'Playland.' Why don't you come too?"

"Me? No way!"

"You're making a mistake, Pinocchio! Believe me, if you don't come, you'll regret it. Where in the world are you going to find a better country for kids? There are no schools there. There are no teachers there. There are no books there. In that blessed land you never study. On Thursday, there's no school, and every week is composed of six Thursdays and one Sunday.[126] Just think—fall break begins on the first day of January and ends on the last day of December. Now that's a country the way I really like it! It's how every civilized country should be! . . ."

"But how do you spend your days in Playland?"

"You spend them playing and having fun from morning till evening. Then in the evening you go to bed, and the next morning you start all over again. What do you think about that?"

"Hmm! . . ." went Pinocchio, and tilted his head from side to side slightly, as if to say: "It's a life I'd like to live too!"

"So, do you want to leave with me? Yes or no? Make up your mind."

"No, no, no, and no again. I've already promised my dear Fairy that I'll become a good boy, and I want to keep my promise. Actually, since I see the sun is going down, I need to leave you right away. So goodbye, and have a good journey."

"Where are you going in such a hurry?"

"Home. My good Fairy wants me to be back before dark."

"Wait another two minutes."

"I'll be too late."

"Just two minutes."

"And what if the Fairy yells at me?"

"Let her yell. When she's had a good yell, she'll shut up," said that rascal Lampwick.

"So how are you going to travel? Alone or with someone else?"

"Alone? There must be more than a hundred kids."

"And will you be traveling on foot?"

"A coach is coming by in a little while to pick me up and take me all the way to within the borders of that glorious country."

"What I wouldn't give for that coach to come by now! . . ."

"Why?"

"So I can see all of you leave together."

"Stay here a little longer and you'll see us."

"No, no. I want to go back home."

"Wait another two minutes."

"I've already lingered too long. The Fairy must be worried about me."

"Poor Fairy! What? Is she afraid the bats will eat you?"

"So then," Pinocchio went on, "are you really sure that in that country there aren't any schools?"

"Not even the trace of one."

"And no teachers either? . . ."

"Not a single one."

"And they don't make you study?"

"Never, ever, ever!"

"What a wonderful country!" said Pinocchio, feeling his mouth starting to water. "What a wonderful country! I've never been there, but I can picture it! . . ."

"Why don't you come too?"

"There's no use in trying to tempt me! I've already promised my good Fairy to become a sensible boy, and I don't want to break my word."

"Well then, goodbye. And give my best to middle school! . . . and to high school too, if you meet it on the way."[127]

"Goodbye, Lampwick. Have a good journey. Have fun and remember your friends from time to time."

That said, the puppet took two steps, as if to leave. But then he stopped, turned around to look at his friend, and asked him:

"But are you really sure that in that country, weeks are composed of six Thursdays and one Sunday?"

"Absolutely sure."

"But do you know for certain that vacation begins on the first of January and finishes at the end of December?"

"Absolutely certain!"

"What a wonderful country!" Pinocchio repeated, and, his mouth having watered so much, he spat. Then, with his mind made up, he added briskly:

"So then—goodbye for real, and have a good journey."

"Goodbye."

"How long before you leave?"

"Not long!"

"I'd just about be capable of waiting."

"And what about the Fairy?"

"At this point, I've already made myself late. And going home an hour sooner or an hour later—it's all the same."

"Poor Pinocchio! And what if the Fairy yells at you?"

"Oh well! I'll let her yell. When she's had a good yell, she'll shut up."

Meanwhile, night—and it was a dark night—had already fallen when all of a sudden they saw a tiny light moving in the distance . . . and heard the sound of harness bells and the call of a bugle so thin and faint that it seemed like the whine of a mosquito!

"Here it is!" shouted Lampwick, getting to his feet.

"What is it?" asked Pinocchio in a whisper.

"It's the coach that's come to pick me up. So. Are you coming? Yes or no?"

"But is it really true," asked the puppet, "that in that country, kids are never under any obligation to study?"

"Never, ever, ever!"

"What a wonderful country! . . . What a wonderful country! . . . What a *wonderful* country! . . ."

After five months of heaven on earth,
Pinocchio—to his great surprise—feels
a nice pair of donkey ears growing
and becomes a little donkey,
with a tail and all.

The coach finally arrived, and it did so without making the slightest noise, for its wheels were wrapped in tow and rags.

It was pulled by twelve pairs of little donkeys, all the same size but with different coats.

Some were gray; others white, others silvery salt and pepper, and yet others were striped with big yellow and turquoise streaks.

But the most unusual thing was this: that those twelve pairs, which is to say those twenty-four little donkeys, instead of having horseshoes like all other animals that are used to pull wagons or carry burdens, were wearing men's ankle boots made of white leather.[128]

And what about the coach driver? . . .

Picture a little man wider than tall, soft and unctuous like a ball of butter,[129] with a small face like a pink apple, a small mouth that was always laughing, and a tiny voice that was thin and affectionate, like that of a cat appealing to the good nature of the mistress of the house.

Kids, as soon as they saw him, fell in love with him and jockeyed to get on his coach and be taken to that true heaven on earth known on the map by the seductive name of Playland.

In fact, the coach was already packed tight with little kids between eight and twelve years old, heaped one on top of the other, like so many anchovies in brine. They were uncomfortable. They were cramped. But nobody said *Ouch!* Nobody complained. The comfort of knowing that in a few hours they were going to arrive in a land where there were no books, no schools, and no teachers made them so happy and acquiescent that they didn't feel the discomfort and the rough treatment, nor any hunger, thirst, or sleepiness.

As soon as the coach stopped, the little man turned to Lampwick, and with a great deal of smirking and fawning, he asked him ingratiatingly:

"Tell me, my handsome boy, do you too want to come to this blessed land?"

"Sure I do."

"But I warn you, my sweet boy, there's no more room in the coach. As you can see, it's all full! . . ."

"Oh well!" replied Lampwick. "If there's no room inside, I'll make do with sitting on the shafts."

And he leapt up and got onto a shaft with his legs astride.

"And what about you, my love? . . ."[130] said the little man, turning to Pinocchio, as smarmy as could be. "What do you want to do? Are you coming with us, or are you going to stay? . . ."

"I'm staying," replied Pinocchio. "I want to go back home. I want to study and I want to do myself proud at school, like all good kids do."

"Much good may it do you!"

"Pinocchio!" Lampwick then said. "Listen to *me*: come away with us and we'll have a ball."

"No, no, no!"

"Come away with us and we'll have a ball," shouted four more voices from inside the coach.

"Come away with us and we'll have a ball," shouted about a hundred voices from inside the coach, all in unison.

"And if I come with you guys, what will my good Fairy say?" asked the puppet, who was starting to weaken and lose his grip on his promise.

"Cross that bridge when you come to it. Don't let such

melancholy thoughts fill your head! Just think, we're going to a land where we'll be free to romp around from morning to night!"

Pinocchio didn't reply, but he sighed. Then he sighed again. Then he sighed a third time. Finally he said:

"Make some room for me. I want to come too! . . ."

"The seats are all taken," replied the little man. "But to show you how happy we are to have you, I can give you my seat on the driver's box."

"And what about you . . . ?"

"I'll go on foot."

"No, really, I won't allow that. I'd rather ride on the back of one of the little donkeys, instead!" shouted Pinocchio.

No sooner said than done, Pinocchio went up to the little donkey on the right of the first pair and made to get on him, but the creature, turning suddenly, butted Pinocchio hard in the stomach and sent him flying with his legs in the air.

Just imagine the raucous, unruly laughter of all those kids looking on.

But the little man didn't laugh. Full of loving care, he approached the rebellious little donkey and, pretending to give him a kiss, bit off half of his right ear.

Meanwhile, Pinocchio got up off the ground in a fury, and leapt onto the back of the poor animal. And the leap was so beautiful that the kids stopped laughing and started shouting "Hurray for Pinocchio!" and applauding so wildly that it seemed they would never stop.

Then, suddenly, the little donkey raised both hind legs and bucked so hard that he flung the poor puppet into the middle of the road onto a heap of gravel.

So then—rowdy laughter all over again. But the little man, instead of laughing, felt seized by such love for that cute, frisky little donkey that, with a kiss, he clean bit off half of his other ear.[131] Then he said to the puppet:

"Go ahead and get back on, and don't be afraid. That little donkey has some bizarre ideas in his head, but I said a couple of sweet words in each of his ears, so I hope I've made him tame and reasonable."

Pinocchio got on, and the coach started to move, but while the little donkeys were galloping and the coach was careering over the stones of the main road, the puppet thought he heard a subdued and barely intelligible voice say to him:

"You poor goon. You wanted to do things your way, but you'll be sorry!"

A little frightened, Pinocchio looked around to try to figure out where the words had come from—but didn't see anyone. The little donkeys were galloping, the coach was careering along, the kids inside were sleeping. Lampwick was snoring like a dormouse, and the little man sitting on the driver's box was singing softly between his teeth:

Everyone sleeps at night
And I never sleep . . .[132]

After another quarter of a mile, Pinocchio heard the same faint little voice say to him:

"Bear this in mind, you silly little clunk—kids who quit studying and turn their backs on books, schools, and teachers to give themselves up entirely to games and fun can't help but come to a miserable end! . . . I know from experience! . . . And I can tell you! A day will come when you too will cry, as I do today . . . But by then it'll be too late! . . ."

At these quietly whispered words, the puppet, more frightened than ever, jumped down off the donkey's back and went over to hold him by the muzzle.

And imagine his reaction when he realized that his little donkey was crying . . . and he was crying just like a boy!

"Hey, Mr. Little Man," shouted Pinocchio to the owner of the coach. "You know something? This donkey is crying."

"Let him cry—he'll laugh when he gets married."[133]

"You haven't, by any chance, taught him how to talk, have you?"

"No. He's learned on his own to mutter a few words, because he spent three years with dogs that were trained."

"Poor thing! . . ."

"Come on! Come on!" said the Little Man. "Let's not waste

our time watching a donkey cry. Get up onto his back again, and let's go. The night is chilly and the way is long."

Pinocchio did as he was told without saying another word. The coach started off on its way again, and in the morning, at the first light of dawn, they arrived happily in Playland.

This country was unlike any other in the world. Its population was composed entirely of kids. The older ones were fourteen, the younger ones barely eight. In the streets it was all merrymaking, romping around, and screaming and yelling—enough to drive you out of your mind! Packs of little scoundrels everywhere. Some were playing the walnut game,[134] others were pitching stones,[135] yet others were playing ball; some were riding high wheel bicycles, others were on wooden horses. Over here, they were playing blind man's buff. Over there, they were chasing after each other. Some dressed as clowns were swallowing lit torches, some were acting, some were singing, some were doing backflips, some were walking on their hands with their legs in the air. This one was rolling a hoop. That one was strutting around dressed as a general with a newspaper helmet and a papier-mâché saber. Some were laughing, some were shouting, some were calling out, some were clapping their hands, some were whistling, some were making the sound of a hen that's just laid an egg. All in all, such pandemonium, such a confused racket like a bunch of sparrows squabbling, such an infernal din that you had to stuff cotton balls in your ears so as not to go deaf. In every piazza you could see little theaters made of canvas, packed with kids from morning to night, and on all the walls of the houses you could read, written in charcoal, such beautiful things as: *Hurrah for toyz* (instead of "toys"), *We don't want no more skools* (instead of "We don't want any more schools"),[136] *Down with Matt Metticks* (instead of "mathematics"), and other gems of that sort.

No sooner had Pinocchio, Lampwick, and all the other kids who had made the journey with the Little Man set foot in the town than they dived into that great hullabaloo, and in a few minutes, as you can well imagine, they all became everyone's friend. Who could have been happier, who could have been merrier than they were?

Amid the endless fun and countless amusements, the hours, days, and weeks passed like so many flashes.

"Oh, what a wonderful life!" Pinocchio would say every time he happened to run into Lampwick.

"You see, then, that I was right?" his friend would reply. "And to think that you didn't want to leave! To think that you had it in your head to go back home to your Fairy and waste time studying! . . . If today you've freed yourself from the bother of books and school, you owe it to me, to my advice, to my caring about you—don't you agree? It's only true friends who do these great favors."

"That's right, Lampwick! If today I'm a truly happy boy, it's all thanks to you. And just think: you know what the teacher would tell me, when he was talking about you? He always used to say: 'Stay away from that rascal Lampwick, because he's a bad influence and will only advise you to do wrong! . . .'"

"Poor old teacher!" replied Lampwick, shaking his head. "I know only too well that he didn't like me and got a kick out of badmouthing me. But I'm big-hearted. I forgive him!"

"What an honorable soul!" Pinocchio said, hugging his friend and placing a kiss on his forehead.

Five months had passed since they had started enjoying this heaven on earth in which they could play and have fun all day long, day after day, without ever setting eyes on a book or a school. But one morning Pinocchio, waking up, had—as they say—a truly awful surprise that put him in a really foul mood.[137]

*Pinocchio grows donkey ears, and then
becomes a real little donkey and starts to bray.*

And what *was* this surprise?

I'll tell you, my dear little readers. The surprise was that Pinocchio, upon waking up, happened quite naturally to scratch his head. And while scratching his head he realized . . .

Just try to guess what he realized?

He realized, to his great astonishment, that his ears had grown by more than a palm's length.

As you know, the puppet had had tiny little ears ever since he was born. So small that they couldn't even be seen with the naked eye! Just imagine his reaction when he realized that, overnight, his ears had grown so long that they seemed like two swamp-reed brushes.[138]

He immediately went to look for a mirror so he could see himself. But since he couldn't find a mirror, he filled the basin that he used to wash his hands and peered into it. He saw what he would never have wanted to see. That is, he saw his reflection embellished by a magnificent pair of donkey ears.

I'll leave it up to you to think about the sorrow, shame, and despair that poor Pinocchio felt!

He started crying, screaming, and banging his head on the wall. But the more he gave himself up to desperation, the more his ears grew. And grew. And grew. And became covered in fur at the tips.

At the sound of those piercing screams, a nice little Marmot[139] who lived on the floor above came into the room. When she saw the puppet in such distress, she asked him kindly:

"What's the matter, dear neighbor?"

"I'm sick, my little Marmot, very sick . . . And I'm sick with an ailment that scares me! Do you know anything about taking a pulse?"

"A little."

"Then see if by chance I have a fever."

The little Marmot lifted her right front paw, and after having felt Pinocchio's pulse, she said to him with a sigh:

"My friend, I'm sorry to have to give you bad news! . . ."

"Which is?"

"You really have an ugly fever! . . ."

"And what kind of a fever would that be?"

"It's Little-Donkey Fever."

"I don't know about that fever!" answered the puppet, who had understood only too well.

"Then I'll explain it to you," the little Marmot went on. "You should be aware that in two or three hours you will no longer be a puppet, or a boy . . ."

"And what will I be?"

"In two or three hours, you will become a real little donkey, like those who pull carts and bring heads of cabbage and lettuce to the market."

"Oh, no! Poor me! Poor me!" cried Pinocchio, grabbing both ears with his hands and pulling and tearing furiously, as if they were someone else's ears.

"My dear," replied the little Marmot in an effort to console him, "what can you do about it? By now, it's your destiny. It's written in the edicts of knowledge that all lazy kids who develop an aversion to books, schools, and teachers, and spend their days in play, games, and fun, must sooner or later end up being turned into so many little donkeys."

"But truly—is that *really* the way it is?" the puppet asked, sobbing.

"Unfortunately, that *is* the way it is! And crying now is pointless. You should have thought about it sooner!"

"But it's not *my* fault. Believe me, my little Marmot, the fault is all Lampwick's! . . ."

"And who is this Lampwick?"

"A schoolmate of mine. I wanted to go back home. I wanted to be obedient. I wanted to keep going to school and do myself proud . . . But Lampwick said: 'Why do you want to go bothering yourself with studying? Why do you want to go to school? . . . Come with me instead, to Playland. There, we won't have to study anymore. There, we'll have fun from morning to night, and we'll always be having a ball.'"

"And why did you follow the advice of that false friend—of that untrustworthy companion?"

"Why? Because, my little Marmot, I'm a puppet with no judgment . . . and no heart. Oh! If only I'd been a bit more good-hearted, I'd have never left that good Fairy who loved me like a mom and did so much for me! . . . And by now I wouldn't be a puppet anymore . . . Instead, I'd be a good little boy, like so many others! But if I run into Lampwick, he'd better watch out! I want to give him a good clobbering! . . ."

And he made to go out. But when he reached the door, he remembered he had donkey ears, and, since he was ashamed of showing them in public, what did he come up with? He took a big cotton nightcap and, sticking it on his head, pulled it all the way down under the tip of his nose.

Then he went out and started looking for Lampwick all over the place.

He looked for him in the streets, in the piazzas, in the little theaters—everywhere. But he couldn't find him. He asked everyone he ran into on the street about him, but no one had seen him.

So he went to look for him at home, and when he got to the front door, he knocked.

"Who is it?" asked Lampwick from inside.

"It's me!" replied the puppet.

"Hold on a little while, and I'll open the door."

After half an hour, the door opened. Just imagine Pinocchio's reaction when, once inside the room, he saw his friend Lampwick with a big cotton nightcap on his head that went all the way down under his nose.

At the sight of the nightcap, Pinocchio almost felt reassured and immediately thought to himself:

"Could my friend be sick with the same ailment that I have? Could it be that he too has Little-Donkey Fever?"

So, pretending he hadn't noticed anything, he asked him with a smile:

"How are you, my dear Lampwick?"

"Very well. Like a mouse in a wheel of parmesan cheese."[140]

"Do you really mean that?"

"Why would I lie to you?"

"I'm sorry, my friend, but why, then, are you wearing that nightcap that completely covers your ears?"

"The doctor ordered it because I hurt my knee. And you, my dear puppet, why are you wearing that cotton nightcap pulled all the way down under your nose?"

"The doctor ordered it because I scraped my foot."[141]

"Oh! Poor Pinocchio! . . ."

"Oh! Poor Lampwick! . . ."

After that, there was a very long silence, during which the two friends did nothing but look at each other teasingly.

At last the puppet, in a mellifluous and flute-like little voice, said to his friend:

"Just out of curiosity, my dear Lampwick, have you ever had something wrong with your ears?"

"¡Never! . . . How about you?"

"Never! But since this morning, my ear has been hurting me."[142]

"I've got the same thing."

"You too? Which ear hurts?"

"Both of them. What about you?"

"Both of them. Could it be the same sickness?"

"I'm afraid so."

"Will you do me a favor, Lampwick?"

"Gladly! With all my heart."

"Will you show me your ears?"

"Why not? But first I want to see yours, my dear Pinocchio."

"No. You go first."

"No, my dear! You first, and then me!"

"Well then," said the puppet at that point, "let's make a deal, like good friends."

"So what's the deal?"

"Let's both take off our nightcaps at the same time. What do you say?"

"Okay."

"So then . . . on your marks!"

And Pinocchio started to count out loud:

"One! Two! Three!"

At the word "Three!" the two boys took their nightcaps off their heads and threw them in the air.

What followed was such a scene that it would seem impossible if it were not true. What happened was that, when Pinocchio and Lampwick saw that they had both been struck by the same misfortune, instead of being mortified and sorrowful, they started to make fun of each other's absurdly overgrown ears, and, after much rowdiness, they ended up laughing wholeheartedly.

They laughed and laughed and laughed—so much that they had to hold their sides. But at the height of their laughter, Lampwick suddenly fell silent, and, swaying and changing color, he said to his friend:

"Help! Help, Pinocchio!"

"What's the matter?"

"Oh my goodness! I can't stand up."

"I can't either," shouted Pinocchio, crying and swaying.

While they were saying this, they both doubled over and fell to the ground on all fours, and, walking on their hands and feet, they started to go in circles and to run around the room. As they ran, their arms became legs, their faces grew long and became muzzles, and their backs became covered in light gray fur, speckled with black.

But do you know what was the worst moment for those two wretches? The worst and most humiliating moment was when they felt a tail growing from behind. Overwhelmed by shame and sorrow, they tried to cry and lament their fate.

It would have been better if they hadn't! Instead of wails of sorrow and lamentation, what they produced was the braying of donkeys. And braying sonorously, they both went *"Hee-haw, hee-haw, hee-haw"* in unison.

Meanwhile, there came a knock at the door, and a voice from outside said:

"Open up! It's the Little Man, the driver of the coach that brought you to this country. Open up right away, or you'll be sorry!"

After he becomes a real donkey,
Pinocchio is taken to be sold and is
bought by the manager of a troupe of
clowns so he can be taught to dance and
jump through hoops. But one evening he
is lamed, and so someone else buys him
to make a drum from his hide.

Seeing that the door wouldn't open up, the Little Man kicked it open violently, and, once inside the room, he said to Pinocchio and Lampwick with that same little laugh of his:

"Well done, boys! You brayed nicely, and I immediately recognized your voices. So that's why I'm here."

When they heard these words, the two little donkeys felt miserable and hung their heads, with their ears down and their tails between their legs.

The Little Man started to stroke them, pet them, and feel them. Then he pulled out a curry comb and gave them a good rubdown. When, after currying them over and over again, he had made them shine like a couple of mirrors, he put a halter on them and took them to the marketplace, hoping to sell them and to make himself a tidy profit.

And in fact the buyers didn't make him wait long.

Lampwick was bought by a farmer whose donkey had died the day before, and Pinocchio was sold to the manager of a troupe of clowns and tightrope performers, who bought him in order to train him and make him jump and dance with the other animals that belonged to the troupe.

So now, my dear little readers, have you understood what the Little Man's fine profession was? From time to time, this horrible, stubby monster with the oh-so-sweet looks would go around the world in his coach. Along the way, he would use promises and endearments to gather all the lazy kids who had an aversion to books and school, and once he had loaded them into his coach, he brought them to Playland, where they would spend their days playing, kicking up a rumpus, and having fun. Then, when those poor duped kids, crazed by playing their hearts out and never studying, turned into so many little donkeys, at that point—all happy and cheerful—he would take possession of them and bring them to fairs and markets to be sold. And in that way, within just a few years, he had made heaps of money and become a millionaire.

What happened to Lampwick, I do not know.[143] But I do know that from the very beginning Pinocchio faced a desperately hard life of toil and mistreatment.

When he was led to the stable, his new master filled the manger with straw for him, but Pinocchio, after just one mouthful, spat it out.

So, grumbling, his master filled the manger with hay for him. But Pinocchio didn't like the hay either.

"Ah! You don't like hay either?" shouted the master furiously. "Don't you worry, you pretty little donkey. If your head is full of fancy notions, I'll take care of getting rid of them! . . ."

And as a way of disciplining him, he whipped him on his legs.

Pinocchio, feeling the sharp pain, started to cry and bray. And as he brayed, he said:

"*Hee-haw, hee-haw.* I can't digest straw! . . ."

"Then eat the hay!" replied his master, who understood donkey dialect[144] very well.

"*Hee-haw, hee-haw.* Hay gives me a stomachache! . . ."

"So then, are you saying I should be feeding a donkey like you chicken breasts and capon in aspic?" asked his master, getting angrier and angrier and whipping him a second time.

At this second whipping, Pinocchio immediately fell silent and, to be on the safe side, said nothing more.

Soon the stable was closed, and Pinocchio was left alone. Since he hadn't eaten for many hours, he started yawning from hunger. And as he yawned, he would open his mouth so wide that it looked like an oven.

In the end, finding nothing else in the manger, he resigned himself to chewing some hay, and having chewed it good and well, he closed his eyes and forced it down.

"This hay doesn't taste bad," he said to himself. "But how much better it would have been if I'd stayed in school! . . . Now, instead of hay, I could be eating the crusty end of a loaf of fresh bread with a nice slice of salami! Oh well! . . ."

The next morning, as he woke up, he immediately looked in the manger for some more hay. But he didn't find any, because he had eaten it all during the night.

So he took a mouthful of shredded hay, but as he chewed it, he had to acknowledge that the taste was nothing like *risotto alla milanese* or *maccheroni alla napoletana*.[145]

"Oh well!" he repeated as he went on chewing. "At least let's hope that my misfortune serves as a lesson to all kids who are disobedient and don't feel like studying. Oh well! . . . Oh well! . . ."

"Oh well, my foot!" shouted his master, coming into the stable at that very moment. "Do you perhaps think, my pretty little donkey, that I bought you just to give you something to eat and drink? I bought you to work and earn me loads of money. So come on, be a good boy! Come with me to the circus and I'll teach you to jump through hoops, to use your head to break open barrels made of paper, and to dance the waltz and the polka on your hind legs.

Poor Pinocchio! Like it or not, he had to learn all these delightful things. But it took him three months of lessons and many whip strokes that scorched his fur off.

Finally, the day arrived when his master could announce a truly extraordinary show. The posters in various colors, pasted up on street corners, read like this:

GRAND GALA SHOW

This evening

THERE WILL TAKE PLACE THE USUAL

AMAZING LEAPS AND FEATS

PERFORMED BY ALL OF THE ARTISTES

and all the horses of both sexes of the company

and moreover

there will be presented for the first time

❋ *the famous* ❋

LITTLE DONKEY PINOCCHIO

also known as

THE DANCING STAR

The theater will be floodlit.

That evening, as you might well imagine, an hour before the show was due to begin, the theater[146] was already jam-packed.

You couldn't get a seat, let alone a ringside seat, to say nothing of a box, even for its weight in gold.

The banks of seats around the ring were teeming with little boys, little girls,[147] and kids of all ages, who were waiting feverishly, in frenzied excitement, to see the famous little donkey Pinocchio dance.

When the first part of the show was over, the manager of the circus, dressed in a black jacket, white riding trousers, and black leather boots over his knees, came out before the packed audience. After bowing deeply, he began with much solemnity the following preposterous speech:

"Honorable members of the audience, my lords and ladies! Your humble undersigned, finding himself passing through this illustrious metropolitan, I desired to conifer[148] upon myself the honor as well as the pleasure of presenting to this brilliant and prodigious audience a celebrated little donkey, who has already had the honor of dancing in front of His Majesty the Emperor of all the Leading Courts of Europe.

"And please, with gracious thanks, help us with your heartening presence and have mercy upon us!"

This speech was received with much laughter and applause. But the applause redoubled and turned into something like a storm when the little donkey Pinocchio appeared in the center of the ring. He was all togged up in his Sunday best. He had a new bridle made of shiny leather, with brass buckles and studs. There were two white camellias[149] behind his ears. His mane was divided up into numerous curls that were tied with little red silk bows. He had a grand gold and silver sash around his middle, and his tail was all braided with light blue and mulberry-red velvet ribbons. All in all, he was a little donkey that you'd fall in love with!

The Ringmaster, introducing him to the audience, added these few words:

"My respectable auditors! I won't stand here and lie to you about the great difficulties I had to abjure in order to understand and subjugate this mammal, while he was grazing freely from mountain to mountain in the plains of the torrid zone. Do observe, I beseech you, how much wildlife oozes from his eyes. And with that said, since all means of domesticating him to live like a civilized quadruped have proved to be in feign, I had to—more than once—resort to the affable dialect of the whip. But every courtesy of mine, instead of making him fond of me, hardened his heart even more toward me. I, however, using the Gallic[150] system, found a small bony Carthage in his skull that the Medicean Faculty in Paris found to be the regenerative bulb of hair—and of the Pyrrhic dance.[151] And that is why I decided to teach him to dance and also to jump through hoops and paper-covered barrels. Behold him! And then be his judge! But before I take my eve of you, allow me, ladies and gentlemen, to invite you to the daytime show tomorrow evening. But in the hypotenuse that the rainy weather threatens a downpour, the show, instead of tomorrow evening, will be postponed to tomorrow morning, at eleven a.m. in the afternoon."

And here the Ringmaster made another very deep bow. Then, turning to Pinocchio, he said:

"Come on, Pinocchio! Before you begin your tricks, say hello to this distinguished audience, to the lords, ladies, and kids!"

Immediately, Pinocchio knelt obediently on the ground and stayed kneeling until the Ringmaster, with a crack of his whip, shouted:

"Walk!"

So the little donkey got up on all four legs and started walking around the ring, keeping a steady pace.

After a short while the Ringmaster shouted:

"Trot!" And Pinocchio, obeying the command, changed his pace to a trot.

"Gallop!" And Pinocchio started to gallop.

"Full speed!" And Pinocchio broke into a headlong dash. But while he was running like a thoroughbred, the Ringmaster raised his arm in the air and fired a gun.

At the sound of the gunshot, the little donkey pretended he had been wounded and fell flat on the floor of the ring, as if he really were dying.

As he pulled himself up from the ground to a storm of applause, of shouts and clapping that reached to the stars, it came naturally to him to lift his head and look up . . . And looking up, he saw a beautiful lady in one of the theater boxes. She was wearing a big gold chain around her neck, from which hung a medallion. On it was painted the portrait of a puppet.

"That portrait is of me! . . . That lady is the Fairy!" Pinocchio said to himself, recognizing her at once. And, giving in to his immense joy, he tried to shout:

"Oh, my dear Fairy! Oh! My dear Fairy! . . ."

But instead of these words, out of his throat came a bray so full and long it made the spectators in the theater—and especially all the kids—burst out laughing.[152]

So the Ringmaster, to teach Pinocchio a lesson and make him understand that it's not good manners to start braying in the spectators' faces, hit him hard on the nose with the handle of his whip.

The poor little donkey stuck out a palm's length of tongue and licked his nose for at least five minutes, maybe hoping in this way to wipe away the pain he felt.

But how immense was his despair when he looked up a second time and saw that the theater box was empty and the Fairy had disappeared! . . .

He almost felt as if he were dying. His eyes filled with tears and he began to weep profusely. But nobody realized—least of all the Ringmaster, who instead cracked his whip and shouted:

"Like a good boy, Pinocchio! Now you're going to show our audience how gracefully you can jump through hoops."

Pinocchio tried two or three times, but every time he got to the hoop, instead of jumping through it, he found it easier to pass underneath. In the end, he jumped and went through it, but unfortunately his hind legs got caught in the hoop, and he fell to the ground on the other side, all in a tangle.

When he got up, he was lame, and could barely make it back to the stable.

"Bring out Pinocchio! We want the little donkey! Bring out the little donkey!" the kids in the orchestra seats were shouting, moved to pity and touched by the heartbreaking turn of events.

But for the rest of the evening, the little donkey was not to be seen again.

The next morning, the veterinarian—the animal doctor—having visited Pinocchio, declared that he would remain lame for the rest of his life.

So the Ringmaster said to his stable boy:

"What am I supposed to do with a lame donkey? He'd only be a no-good freeloader. Take him to the marketplace and re-sell him."

Once they got to the marketplace, they immediately found a buyer, who asked the stable boy:

"How much do you want for that little lame donkey?"

"Twenty *lire*."[153]

"I'll give you twenty *soldi*. Don't go thinking I'm buying him to put him to use. I'm just buying him for his hide. I can see he's got a very tough hide,[154] and I want to use it to make a drum for my town's band."

I'll leave you to think, kids, what a great pleasure it was for poor Pinocchio when he heard that he was destined to become a drum!

The fact is that the buyer, as soon as he had paid the twenty *soldi*, led the little donkey to the seashore. And having tied a rock to his neck and attached one of his legs to a rope that he held in his hand, he shoved him and threw him into the water.

Pinocchio, with that big stone tied to his neck, went straight to the bottom. The buyer, holding on tight to the rope, sat down on a rock and gave the little donkey all the time he needed to drown, so that he could then strip off his hide.

Thrown into the sea, Pinocchio is eaten by fish
and goes back to being a puppet, as before.
But while he is swimming to save himself,
he is swallowed by the terrible Shark.

After the little donkey had been underwater for fifty minutes, the buyer, who was having a conversation with himself, said:

"By now, my poor little lame donkey must be well and truly drowned. So let's pull him back up again and make that nice drum with his hide."

And he started to pull the rope he had tied to Pinocchio's leg. He pulled and pulled and pulled, and at the end he saw, breaking the surface of the water . . . guess? Instead of a dead little donkey, he saw, breaking the surface of the water, a live puppet who was wriggling like an eel.

At the sight of that wooden puppet, the poor man thought he was dreaming and just stood there dazed with his mouth open and his eyes bulging out of his head.

After recovering a little from his initial amazement, he said, weeping and stammering:

"So where is the little donkey I threw into the sea? . . ."

"*I'm* that little donkey!" replied the puppet, laughing.

"You?"

"Me!"

"Why, you little rogue! Are you trying to make a fool of me?"

"Make a fool of you? On the contrary, my dear master, I'm serious."

"But how come you, who just a short while ago were a little

donkey, now, after being in the water, have become a wooden puppet? . . ."

"It must be the effect of the salt water. This is the sort of trick the sea plays."

"Watch out, puppet! Watch out! . . . Don't think you're going to have fun at my expense! You'll be sorry if I lose my patience! . . ."

"Well, master, do you want to know the real story? Untie my leg and I'll tell you."

Curious to know the real story, that simpleton of a buyer immediately undid the knot in the rope that kept Pinocchio tied, and the puppet, finding himself as free as a bird in the sky, began to tell him the following:

"The thing you need to know is that I used to be a wooden puppet, the way I am now, and I was just on the point of becoming a boy, like so many others in the world. But because of my reluctance to study and because I listened to the wrong kind of friends, I ran away from home . . . And one fine day I woke up to find that I had turned into a donkey, complete with ears . . . and even a tail! . . . What shame I felt! . . . Such shame, my dear master, that I hope the blessed Saint Anthony will protect you from ever experiencing it![155] I was taken to be sold at the donkey market and bought by the manager of a circus that had performing horses. He'd gotten it into his head to make me into a great dancer and hoop jumper. But one evening, during a performance in the theater, I had a bad fall, and both my legs were crippled. So the manager, having no use for a lame donkey, sent me to be resold, and I was bought by you! . . ."

"Unfortunately! I paid twenty *soldi* for you. So now who's going to give me back my twenty *soldi*?"

"And why did you buy me? You bought me to make a drum with my hide! . . . A drum! . . ."

"Unfortunately! So now where will I find another hide? . . ."

"Don't despair, master. There are lots of little donkeys in this world!"

"Tell me, you impertinent little scoundrel, does your story end here?"

"No," replied the puppet. "There are a couple more words, and then it's finished. After you bought me, you led me here to kill me. But then, giving in to feelings of humane compassion, you chose to tie a rock to my neck and drop me to the bottom of the sea. The delicacy of your feelings does you great credit, and I will forever be grateful to you for it. But you see, my dear master, you didn't take the Fairy into consideration."

"And who is this Fairy?"

"She's my mom, who is like all the good moms that love their children dearly and never lose sight of them and help them lovingly through every misfortune, even when their kids, because of their recklessness and misbehavior, deserve to be abandoned and left to their fate. So—I was saying—the good Fairy, as soon as she saw me in danger of drowning, sent an endless shoal of fish to surround me, and since they really did think I was a dead donkey, they started to eat me! And they were taking such big bites!! I would never have thought fish were even greedier[156] than kids! . . . Some ate my ears, some my muzzle, others my neck and mane, yet others the skin on my legs and the fur on my back . . . And among them there was a little fish that was so polite he even ate my tail."

"From now on," said the horrified buyer, "I swear I'll never eat fish again. I wouldn't be so happy to open up a fried red mullet or a hake and find a donkey tail in its belly."

"I'm with you," replied the puppet, laughing. "In any case, you should know that when the fish had finished eating all that layer of donkey that covered me from head to foot, naturally they got to the bone . . . or, better said, they got to the wood—because, as you can see, I'm made entirely of very hard wood. But after they took the first bites, those greedy fish realized immediately that this was no flesh for their teeth, and, nauseated by this indigestible food, they left—some going this way, others that way—without so much as a thank-you. And that is the story of how it was that, when you pulled up the rope, you found a live puppet instead of a dead donkey."

"I couldn't care less about your story," shouted the buyer in a rage. "All I know is that I spent twenty *soldi* to buy you, and I want my money back. You know what I'm going to do? I'm going to take you to the market all over again and sell you by weight as seasoned wood for lighting a fire."

"Go ahead and resell me. I'm happy with that," said Pinocchio.

But in so saying, he took a big leap and splashed into the water. Swimming happily away from the beach, he shouted to the poor buyer:

"Goodbye, master. If you need a hide to make a drum, bear me in mind."

And he laughed and kept on swimming. After a while, turning back, he shouted more loudly:

"Goodbye, master. If you need some seasoned firewood, bear me in mind."

The fact is that in the blink of an eye he had gone so far that you could barely see him anymore. That is, on the surface of the water you could see only a tiny little black dot that from time to time lifted its legs out of the water and turned somersaults and took leaps, like a dolphin in a cheerful mood.

As Pinocchio swam on aimlessly, he saw in the middle of the sea a rock that looked like white marble. And on top of the rock he saw a pretty little goat who was bleating lovingly and motioning him to come close.

The most unusual thing was this: the little goat's wool, instead of being white, or black, or dappled in two colors, like that of other goats, was blue—a startling blue, which looked very much like the pretty Little Girl's hair.

I'll leave it to you to ponder whether poor Pinocchio's heart started to beat faster! Redoubling his strength and energy, he started to swim toward the white rock and was already halfway when, out of the water, there emerged the horrible head of a sea monster that made straight for him, its mouth wide open like an abyss, showing three rows of teeth that would have been terrifying even if you were just to see them painted.

And do you know who that sea monster was?

That sea monster was none other than the gigantic Shark that has been mentioned more than once in this story. Because of its carnage and insatiable voracity, it was known as "the Attila[157] of fish and fisherfolk."

Imagine poor Pinocchio's terror at the sight of the monster. He tried to move out of its way, to change direction—to escape. But that immense gaping mouth kept getting closer. At the speed of lightning.

"Hurry, Pinocchio, for pity's sake!" bleated the pretty little goat as loudly as she could.

Pinocchio was swimming desperately with his arms, his chest, his legs, and his feet.

"Faster, Pinocchio—the monster is getting closer! . . ."

And Pinocchio, summoning all his strength, redoubled his efforts to go fast.

"Watch out, Pinocchio! . . . The monster's catching up! . . . It's there! . . . It's almost there! . . . Hurry, for pity's sake, or you'll be finished! . . ."

And Pinocchio kept swimming as fast as ever—on and on and on, like a bullet from a rifle. He had almost reached the rock and the little goat was leaning right out over the water, reaching out to him with her front legs to help him out of the sea . . . But . . . But it was too late! The monster had caught up with him. Drawing in its breath, it sucked in the poor puppet the way you would gulp down a raw chicken egg.[158] And it swallowed him with so much violence and greed that Pinocchio, falling down into the belly of the Shark, took such an unseemly blow that it left him dazed for a quarter of an hour.

When he recovered his wits, he couldn't even figure out what world he was in. All around him was darkness. Everywhere. But it was such a deep, black darkness that it felt to him as if he had stuck his head into a full bottle of ink. He listened for the merest sound—but didn't hear a thing. He could only feel, from time to time, great gusts of wind hitting his face. At first he couldn't understand where the wind was coming from, but then he realized it was coming from the monster's lungs. Because, you see, the Shark suffered from bad asthma, and when he breathed, it really felt like the North Wind was blowing.[159]

At first, Pinocchio tried to find a way to summon up a tiny bit of courage, but when he got proof and yet more proof that he was trapped in the belly of the sea monster, he began to weep and shout, and as he cried he said:

"Help! Help! Oh poor me! Isn't there anyone who can come and save me?"

"Who do you think is going to save you, you poor wretch? . . ." said an ugly, hollow voice that came out of the darkness sounding like an untuned guitar.[160]

"Who's that speaking?" asked Pinocchio, feeling himself freeze in fear.

"It's me! I'm a poor Tuna who was swallowed by the Shark at the same time as you. And what kind of fish are *you*?"

"I've got nothing to do with fish. I'm a puppet."

"So then, if you're not a fish, why did you let yourself be swallowed by the monster?"

"I didn't *let* myself be swallowed. It was *he* who swallowed *me*! And now what are we supposed to do here in the dark? . . ."

"Resign ourselves to our fate and wait for the Shark to digest us both! . . ."

"But I don't want to be digested!" shouted Pinocchio, starting to weep again.

"Neither do I," replied the Tuna. "But I'm pretty much of a philosopher, and I console myself by thinking that if you're born a tuna, there's more dignity to dying in water than in oil! . . ."[161]

"Nonsense!" shouted Pinocchio.

"Mine is an opinion," replied the Tuna. "And as political tunas say, opinions must be respected!"

"In any case . . . I want to get out of here . . . I want to escape."

"Then escape, if you can manage to! . . ."

"Is this Shark that swallowed us very large?" asked the puppet.

"Are you kidding? His body is more than half a mile long, not counting the tail."

While they were having this conversation in the dark, Pinocchio thought he saw a sort of dim light far, far away.

"What could that tiny light be so far, far away?" he said.

"It must be some companion in misfortune who—like us— is waiting to be digested! . . ."

"I want to go see him. Maybe it's some old fish who can teach me how to escape?"

"I do hope so with all my heart, my dear puppet."

"Goodbye, Tuna."

"Goodbye, puppet. And good luck."

"Where will we meet again? . . ."

"Who knows? . . . It's best not even to think about it!"

In the belly of the Shark,
Pinocchio meets . . . Whom does he meet?
Read this chapter and find out.

After he had said goodbye to his good friend the Tuna, Pinocchio stumbled, groping in the dark, and started to walk, feeling his way along the Shark's insides, taking one step after the
other as he made his way toward that tiny faint light he could
see glimmering far, far away.

And while he was walking, he could feel his feet slushing
along in a pool of greasy, slippery water. The water smelled so
strongly of fried fish that he felt as if he were halfway through
Lent.[162]

The farther he went on, the clearer and more distinct the
faint light became until, after walking and walking, in the end
he arrived. And when he got there . . . what did he find? You'll
never get it right, even if I give you a thousand guesses. He
found a small table, set for a meal. On it was a lit candle stuck
in a green glass bottle and, sitting at the table, was a little old
man who was completely white, as if he were made of snow or
whipped cream. He was sitting there slurping as he ate some
little live fish—so alive that sometimes, as he was eating them,
they would escape from his mouth.[163]

At the sight of this, poor Pinocchio was filled with a joy so
great and unexpected that he was within a hair's breadth of
going delirious. He wanted to laugh. He wanted to weep. He
wanted to say a multitude of things—and instead he was
whimpering in confusion and stammering words that were in-
complete and incoherent. In the end, he managed to let out a

cry of joy, and opening his arms wide, he threw them around the little old man's neck and started to shout:

"Oh, my dear Daddy! I've found you at last! I'll never leave you again! Never, ever, ever!"

"So my eyes do not deceive me?" replied the little old man, rubbing his eyes. "So you really *are* my dear Pinocchio?"

"Yes! Yes! It's me—really me! And you've already forgiven me, haven't you? Oh! My dear Daddy! You're so good! . . . And to think that I, instead . . . Oh, but if you only knew what misfortunes have rained down on me, and how many things went wrong for me! Just think, the day that you, my poor Daddy, sold your coat to buy me my spelling book so I could go to school, I ran away to go see the puppet show, and the puppeteer wanted to put me on the fire so I could cook his roast mutton, and he was the one who gave me five gold coins so I could bring them home to you, but I ran into the Cat and the Fox, who took me to the Red Crayfish Inn, where they ate like a couple of wolves, and I left on my own at night and ran into murderers who started running after me, and I fled, and they chased me, and I fled, and they kept chasing, and I fled until they hanged me from a branch of the Big Oak, where the beautiful blue-haired Little Girl sent for me to be collected with a little carriage, and the doctors, after they visited me, said at once, 'If he's not dead, it's a sign that he's still alive,' and so I couldn't help telling a lie, and my nose started to grow, and it wouldn't fit through the door of the room, which is why I went with the Fox and the Cat to bury the four gold coins, 'cause one I had spent at the Inn, and the Parrot started laughing, and instead of two thousand gold coins I didn't find anything anymore, so the judge when he learned I'd been robbed had me sent straight to jail, to give the robbers some satisfaction, from where, while I was coming away, I saw a nice bunch of grapes in a field, so I got caught in a trap and the farmer—and he had every right to do so—put a dog collar on me so I'd guard the chicken coop, and he recognized my innocence and let me go, and the Snake, with smoke coming out of its tail, started to laugh and a vein on its chest tore open, and so I went back to the house of the beautiful Little Girl who was dead, and the Pigeon who saw that I was crying said to me: 'I saw your dad making himself a little boat to go look for you,' and I said, 'Oh, if only I had wings too,' and he said, 'Do you want to go see your dad?' and I said, 'I wish! But who's going to take me there?' and he said, 'I will,' and I said, 'How?' and he said, 'Get on my back,' and so we flew all night, and then in the morning all the fishermen who were looking out to sea told me: 'There's a poor man in a little boat who's about to drown,' and from far away I recognized you immediately because my heart was telling me, and I signaled to you to come back to the beach . . ."

"I recognized you too," said Geppetto. "And I would have gladly gone back to the beach—but how? The sea was very rough and a big wave turned my boat over. So a horrible Shark that was nearby, as soon as he saw me in the water, rushed straight toward me, stuck his tongue out and pulled me in just the way I was, and swallowed me like a tortellino from Bologna."[164]

"And how long have you been trapped in here?" asked Pinocchio.

"From that day on. It must be about two years now . . . Two years, my dear Pinocchio, that have felt like two centuries!"

"And how did you manage to survive? And how did you find the candle? And the matches to light it—who gave them to you?"

"I'll tell you the whole story. So, you see, the same storm that turned my boat over sunk a freighter too. The sailors all survived, but the ship went down, and the same Shark, which had an excellent appetite that day, after having swallowed me, swallowed the ship as well."

"What? He swallowed it all in one mouthful? . . ." asked Pinocchio in astonishment.

"All in one mouthful. And he only spat out the main mast because it had gotten stuck between his teeth, like a fishbone. Luckily for me, that cargo ship was not just full of canned meat, but also of rusks—you know, slices of toasted bread—bottles of wine, raisins, cheese, coffee, sugar, tallow candles, and waxed matches. With this gift of God I've been able to live for two years, but now I'm down to the last scrapings. Now there is nothing left in the pantry, and this candle here that you see lit is the last I have left . . ."

"So what happens when it burns out? . . ."

"Then, my dear boy, we'll both be left in the dark."

"That means, my dear Daddy," replied Pinocchio, "there's no time to waste. We need to think right now about how we escape . . ."[165]

"Escape? . . . But how?"

"We'll get out through the mouth of the Shark, jump into the sea, and swim."

"That's easily said, but—my dear Pinocchio—I don't know how to swim."[166]

"So what? . . . You'll get on my shoulders. I'm a good swimmer, and I'll bring you safe and sound to the shore."

"You're kidding yourself, my dear boy!" replied Geppetto, shaking his head and smiling ruefully. "Do you really think it's possible that a puppet like you, barely a meter tall, could have enough strength to swim with me on his shoulders?"

"Just try it and you'll see! In any case, if it's written in the heavens above that we must die, at least we'll have the immense consolation of dying in each other's arms."

And without another word, Pinocchio took the candle and, going ahead to light the way, said to his dad:

"Follow me, and don't be afraid."

And so they walked quite a long way, and went the whole length of the body and the stomach of the Shark. But when they reached the place where the great throat of the monster began, they were smart enough to stop and have a look and decide on the right moment to escape.

Now you must bear in mind that since the Shark was very old and suffered from asthma and heart palpitations, he was forced to sleep with his mouth open. So Pinocchio, standing at the bottom of the throat and looking up through the enormous, wide-open mouth, could see a good portion of the sky, filled with stars and with the beautiful light of the moon.

"This is the right moment to escape," he whispered, turning to his dad. "The Shark is sleeping like a log, the sea is calm, and you can see as clearly as in the daytime. So follow me, Daddy, and soon we'll be safe."

No sooner said than done, they went up the throat of the sea monster, and once they got into that immense mouth, they started to tiptoe along the tongue—a tongue so wide and so long that it seemed like a drive leading through a park.[167] And they were just about to make their big jump into the sea and start swimming when, right at that moment, the Shark sneezed. And as he sneezed he gave such a violent jerk that Pinocchio and Geppetto found themselves bounced all the way down again—flung back into the monster's stomach.

So violent was the impact of their fall that the candle went out, and father and son were left in the dark.

"And now what do we do? . . ." asked Pinocchio, suddenly turning serious.

"Now, my boy, we are really and truly done for."

"Why done for? Give me your hand, Daddy, and be careful not to slip! . . ."

"Where are you taking me?"

"We have to try again. Come with me, and don't be afraid."

That said, Pinocchio took his dad by the hand, and, tiptoe-ing the whole way, together they went up the monster's throat. Then they went the whole length of the tongue and climbed over the three rows of teeth. But before they took their great leap, the puppet said to his dad:

"Get on my shoulders and hold on really tight. I'll take care of the rest."

As soon as Geppetto had settled himself onto his son's shoulders,[168] Pinocchio, with utter confidence, jumped into the water and started swimming. The sea was calm and as smooth as oil. The moon was shining in all its brightness. And the Shark kept sleeping—in such a deep sleep that not even a cannon shot would have woken him.

Finally, Pinocchio ceases to be a puppet and becomes a boy.

As Pinocchio was swimming fast to get to the beach, he realized that his dad, who was riding on his back and had his legs half in the water, was trembling violently, as if the poor man were suffering an attack of malaria.[170]

Was he shaking because he was afraid or because he was cold? Who knows? . . . Maybe a bit of both. But Pinocchio thought the shaking was from fear. So to comfort him, he said:

"Hang in there, Dad! In a few minutes we'll reach land, and then we'll be safe."

"But where is the blessed land?" asked the little old man, getting more and more apprehensive and squinting the way that tailors do when they thread their needles. "Here I am looking all around, but all I can see is sea and sky."

"But I can see the shore as well,"[171] said the puppet. "Just so you know, I'm like a cat: I can see better at night than during the day."

Poor Pinocchio was pretending to be in a good mood, but instead . . . instead he was starting to grow disheartened, because he was losing strength, his breath was getting heavy and wheezy . . . in short, he couldn't last much longer, and the beach was still far away.

He swam on for as long as he still had breath in him. Then he turned his head toward Geppetto, and said between gasps:

"My dear Dad . . . save yourself![172] . . . because I'm dying! . . ."

Father and son were about to drown when they heard a voice that sounded like an untuned guitar say:

"Who is it that's dying?"

"It's me and my poor dad! . . ."

"That voice! I recognize it! You're Pinocchio! . . ."

"That's right! And who are you?"

"I'm the Tuna, your fellow prisoner inside the Shark."

"And how did you escape?"

"I followed your example. You're the one who showed me the way. And after you did, I escaped too."

"My dear Tuna, you've turned up at just the right time! I beg you, in the name of the love you have for your baby-tuna children—help us, or we're doomed."

"I'd be happy to! With all my heart. Both of you catch hold of my tail and let yourselves be led. In four minutes I'll take you to shore."

Geppetto and Pinocchio, as you may well imagine, immediately accepted the invitation. But instead of catching hold of his tail, they figured it would actually be more comfortable to sit on the Tuna's back.

"Are we too heavy?" Pinocchio asked him.

"Heavy? Not at all—it feels like I have a couple of empty seashells on my back," replied the Tuna, who was so big and strongly built that he looked like a two-year-old calf.

Once they got to shore, Pinocchio was the first to jump onto the ground so he could help his dad do the same. Then he turned to the Tuna and, choking up with emotion, said:

"My dear friend, you saved my dad! I'm at a loss for words to thank you enough! Allow me, at least, to give you a kiss as a token of my eternal gratitude! . . ."

The Tuna stuck his nose out of the water, and Pinocchio, kneeling to the ground, placed a kiss that was full of affection on his mouth.[173] The poor Tuna, who wasn't used to such displays of spontaneous and heartfelt tenderness, felt so moved that he pulled his head back under the water and disappeared, ashamed to be seen crying like a baby.

In the meantime, the sun had risen.

So Pinocchio offered his arm to Geppetto, who barely had the strength to stand on his feet, and said:

"Lean on my arm, my dear Daddy, and let's go. We'll walk

nice and slowly, like ants do, and when we're tired we'll rest along the way."

"And where are we supposed to go?" asked Geppetto.

"In search of a house or a shack, where they might spare us a crust of bread and some straw to use as a bed."

They had not gone more than a hundred paces when they saw two ugly-looking lowlifes sitting on the roadside, begging.

It was the Cat and the Fox.[174] But you could hardly recognize them from how they used to be. Just imagine—the Cat, because he kept pretending he was blind, had ended up going blind for real. And the Fox, who had grown old, was covered in patches of ringworm and paralyzed down one side. He didn't even have his tail anymore. Such is life. That miserable little thief, who had fallen into the most wretched poverty, had one fine day even been forced to sell his beautiful tail to a traveling salesman, who bought it to make himself a fly whisk.

"Oh, Pinocchio," cried the Fox in a whining voice. "Do you have anything to spare for a couple of poor invalids?"

"Invalids!" repeated the Cat.

"Goodbye, you jokers!"[175] replied the puppet. "You cheated me once, and now you're not going to get your claws into me again."

"Believe me, Pinocchio—these days we're poor and wretched for real!"

"For real!" repeated the Cat.

"If you're poor, you deserve it. Remember the proverb 'Stolen money never bears fruit.' Goodbye, you jokers!"

"Have pity on us! . . ."

"On us! . . ."

"Goodbye, you jokers! Remember the proverb 'The devil's flour all turns to bran.'"

"Don't abandon us! . . ."

"Us!" repeated the Cat.

"Goodbye, you jokers! Remember the proverb 'Those who steal their neighbor's cape usually die without a shirt.'"

And so saying, Pinocchio and Geppetto simply continued on their way along the road until, after another hundred paces, at the end of a lane that ran through the fields, they saw a nice hut made entirely of straw, its roof covered with tiles and bricks.

"There must be someone living in that hut," said Pinocchio. "Let's go and knock."

So they went and knocked on the door.

"Who is it?" said a little voice from inside.

"It's a poor dad and a poor son, with no bread and no roof over their heads," replied the puppet.

"Turn the key and the door will open," said the same little voice.

Pinocchio turned the key, and the door opened. As soon as they were inside, they looked this way and that, but they couldn't see anyone.

"So where's the owner of the hut?" asked Pinocchio in amazement.

"Here I am—up here!"

Father and son immediately looked up toward the ceiling, and, on a little beam, they saw the Talking Cricket.

"Oh! My dear little Cricket," said Pinocchio, greeting him politely.

"So now you call me your 'dear little Cricket,' do you? But remember when you threw the handle of a mallet at me to get me out of your house? . . ."

"You're right, dear little Cricket! Make me get out as well . . . throw the handle of a mallet at me too. But have pity on my poor dad . . ."

"I'll have pity on the dad and on the son as well. But I wanted to remind you of your ill-treatment of me so that you would understand that in this world, when we can, we need to be kind to everyone if we want to be treated with the same sort of kindness in our times of need."

"You're right, dear little Cricket! You're absolutely right, and I'll bear in mind the lesson you've taught me. But tell me—how did you manage to buy yourself this nice hut?"

"It was given to me yesterday by a delightful goat whose wool was a beautiful blue."

"And where did the goat go?" Pinocchio asked with intense curiosity.

"I don't know."

"And when will she be back? . . ."

"She will never come back. Yesterday she left, downhearted and depressed, and her bleating sounded as if she were saying: 'Poor Pinocchio . . . I'll never see him again now . . . By now, the Shark will already have devoured him! . . .'"

"Is that what she really said? . . . So then it was her! . . . It was her! . . . It was my dear Fairy! . . ." shouted Pinocchio, starting to weep and sob profusely.

When he had wept his heart out, he dried his eyes, and having prepared a nice bed of straw, he laid old Geppetto on it. Then he asked the Talking Cricket:

"Tell me, dear little Cricket, where could I find a glass of milk for my poor dad?"

"Three fields away from here, you'll find John Joe, who grows vegetables and keeps cows. Go over to his place, and you'll find the milk you're looking for."

Pinocchio immediately rushed over to John Joe's, but the farmer said:

"How much milk do you want?"

"I want a glassful."

"A glass of milk costs one *soldo*. Why don't you start by giving me the *soldo*?"

"I don't have even one cent," replied a mortified and disconsolate Pinocchio.

"Not good, my dear puppet," replied the man. "If you don't have even a cent, I don't have even a drop of milk."

"Oh well!" said Pinocchio, and he turned as if to leave.

"Wait a minute," said John Joe. "We could make an arrangement. Would you be prepared to turn the water wheel?"

"What's a water wheel?"

"It's that wooden mechanism that's used to draw water up from the rainwater tank for the vegetables."

"I can try . . ."

"So, you draw a hundred buckets of water and I'll reward you with a glass of milk."

"All right."

John Joe led the puppet to the vegetable garden and showed

him how to turn the water wheel. Pinocchio set himself to work right away, but before he had drawn the hundred buckets of water, he was covered in sweat. He had never worked so hard.

"Until now, this hard work of turning the water wheel has been my little donkey's job," said the farmer. "But now the poor animal is dying."

"Will you take me to see him?" said Pinocchio.

"Sure."

As soon as Pinocchio entered the stable, he saw a pretty little donkey lying on the straw, all skin and bones from hunger and overwork. After he had had a careful look at him, he became deeply troubled and said to himself:

"But I know that little donkey! His face isn't new to me!"

And kneeling down close to him, he asked in donkey dialect:

"Who are you?"

In response, the little donkey opened his dying eyes and, stammering in the same dialect, answered:

"I'm Lamp . . . wick . . ."

Then he closed his eyes again and breathed his last.

"Oh! Poor Lampwick!" said Pinocchio in a low voice, and took a handful of straw to dry off a tear that was running down his face.

"You're that moved because of a donkey that hasn't cost you a thing?" said the farmer. "So what should *I* do, after having paid good money for him?"

"I'll explain . . . He was a friend of mine! . . ."

"A *friend* of yours?"

"A schoolmate of mine! . . ."

"What?!" shouted John Joe, bursting into laughter. "You had donkeys for schoolmates? . . . I can just imagine the good education you must have had! . . ."

Feeling mortified by those words, the puppet didn't reply. Instead, he took his glass of milk that was still almost warm and went back to the hut.

From that day on, and for more than five months, Pinocchio would get up every morning before dawn to go turn the water wheel and earn the glass of milk that was so good for his dad's delicate health. But that wasn't enough for him, because in his spare time he learned to weave reeds and make baskets of various kinds. With the little money he made from them, he very judiciously took care of all their daily expenses. Among other things, he made, all by himself, an elegant little handcart to take his dad for a stroll on days when the weather was fine, so that Geppetto could get a breath of fresh air.

In the evenings, he would practice reading and writing. In the town nearby, he had bought for a few cents a large book that was missing its frontispiece and index, and with it he did his reading. As far as writing went, he used a twig that was sharpened like a pen, and since he had neither an ink bottle nor ink, he would dip the twig into a little bottle filled with the juice of berries and cherries.

The fact is that because of his readiness to use his ingenuity, work hard, and forge ahead, not only did he manage to give his poor, sickly father an almost comfortable life, but he was also able to put aside forty *soldi* to buy himself a new little outfit.

One morning he said to his father:

"I'm going to the market nearby to buy myself a little jacket, a hat, and a pair of shoes. When I come back home," he added with a laugh, "I'll be dressed so well you'll mistake me for a fine gentleman."

So he left the house and started running, as happy and cheerful as could be, when all of a sudden he heard someone call him by his name. He turned around and saw a pretty snail coming out from a hedge.

"Don't you recognize me?" asked the Snail.

"I do and I don't . . ."

"Don't you remember that snail who was living with the Blue-haired Fairy? Don't you recall that time when I came down to bring you some light and you got stuck with your foot in the front door?"

"I remember everything," cried Pinocchio. "Tell me at once, my beautiful little Snail, where did you last see my good Fairy? What is she doing? Has she forgiven me? Does she still remember me? Does she still love me? Is she very far from here? Could I go visit her?"

With her customary composure the Snail answered all these questions that the puppet had asked so precipitously and without taking a breath:

"My dear Pinocchio, the poor Fairy has been lying ill in a poorhouse bed for a very long time! . . ."

"In a poorhouse? . . ."

"Unfortunately so. Struck down by countless misfortunes, she has fallen seriously ill and doesn't have anything left with which to buy even a crust of bread."

"Really? . . . Oh, what deep pain your news gives me! Oh! Poor dear Fairy! Poor dear Fairy! . . . If I had a million, I'd run to bring it to her . . . But all I have is forty *soldi* . . . Here they are: I was just going to buy myself a new outfit. Take them, Snail—go right away and give them to my good Fairy!"

"And what about your new outfit? . . ."

"What do I care about a new outfit? I'd even sell the rags I'm wearing to be able to help her! Go, Snail, and hurry! Come back in two days, because I hope to be able to give you a few more *soldi*. Until now I've worked to provide for my dad. Starting today I'll work five hours longer to provide for my good mom too. Goodbye, Snail, and I'll be expecting you in two days."

Contrary to her usual habit, the Snail set off running like a lizard under the hot August sun.

When Pinocchio got home again, his dad asked him:

"What about your new outfit?"

"I couldn't find one that fit. Oh well! . . . I'll buy one some other time."

That evening Pinocchio, instead of staying up until ten, stayed up until it had already struck midnight, and instead of making eight reed baskets, he made sixteen.

Then he went to bed and fell asleep. While he was sleeping, he thought he saw the Fairy in a dream. She was smiling and she looked beautiful and, after giving him a kiss, she said:

"Good boy, Pinocchio! Because of your kind heart I will forgive all of your bad behavior up until now. Kids who lovingly care for their parents in times of illness and distress always deserve great praise and lots of love, even if they can't be held up as models of obedience and good behavior. Use good judgment in the future, and you will be happy."

At this point, the dream ended, and Pinocchio woke up with his eyes wide open.

Now, just imagine his amazement when, upon waking, he realized he was no longer a wooden puppet but instead had become a boy like all the others.[176] He glanced all around and, instead of the same old straw walls of the hut, he saw a pretty little room, furnished and decorated with a simplicity that was almost elegant. Jumping down off the bed, he found some nice new clothes ready for him, a new hat, and a new pair of leather ankle boots[177] that fit just beautifully.

As soon as he got dressed, it came naturally to him to put his hands in his pockets. From one, he pulled out a small ivory coin purse, on which were written the following words: "The Blue-haired Fairy returns the forty *soldi* to her dear Pinocchio and thanks him so very much for his kind heart." When he opened the billfold, instead of the forty copper *soldi*, he saw forty glistening gold coins, all freshly minted.

Then he went to look at himself in the mirror—and he looked as if he were someone else. He no longer saw the same old reflected image of a wooden marionette.[178] Instead, he saw the image of a smart, lively, beautiful child with brown hair and blue eyes who was as happy and joyful as a spring lamb.

Amid all these wonderful things that were happening one after the other, Pinocchio couldn't tell if he was truly awake or still dreaming with his eyes open.

"And where's my dad?" he shouted all of a sudden. Going into the room next door, he found old Geppetto in a good mood and as healthy and sprightly as he had once been. He had resumed his trade as a woodcarver and was intent on designing a beautiful frame with leaves, flowers, and the miniature heads of various animals.

"I'm curious, Daddy. How can this sudden change be explained?" Pinocchio asked him, throwing his arms around his neck and smothering him with kisses.

"This sudden change in our home is all thanks to you," Geppetto said.

"Why thanks to me? . . ."

"Because when kids stop being bad and start being good, they also bring a new and joyous air into their families."

"And where do you think the old wooden Pinocchio has gone?"

"There he is—over there!" replied Geppetto, and he motioned toward a large puppet that was propped up in a chair, his head turned to one side, his arms dangling and his legs crossed and bent at the knees. It seemed miraculous that he could stay upright.

Pinocchio turned to look at him, and after he had looked at him for a little while, he said to himself with deep satisfaction:

"How funny I was when I was a puppet! And how happy I am now to have become a good little kid! . . ."[179]

Notes

CHAPTER I

1. By opening his story in this very traditional way, Carlo Collodi was also sending a message, if only to a restricted circle of cognoscenti: that the story that followed was not in fact just for children. Collodi was also a satirical journalist. *C'era una volta*, the Italian equivalent of "Once upon a time," was a sort of in-joke among satirical writers in his circle: a phrase he and they often used to start articles that were only superficially fairy tales. Collodi himself was quoted in *La Lente* in 1856 as having said: "Hey! Have you mistaken us for a bunch of kids with that 'Once upon a time'? . . . No. No. Hold on . . . I am not telling you a fairy tale as would seem to be the case . . ."

2. This is a remarkably provocative association to make at the beginning of a story in 1881. Italy had been unified just eleven years earlier under a king, Vittorio Emanuele II. The extension of monarchical rule to the whole of Italy sat uneasily with the many republicans who had worked, and in many cases risked their lives, in the cause of Unification. Carlo Lorenzini, the writer behind the pseudonym Carlo Collodi, who fought in the First (1848–49) and Second (1859–61) Wars of Independence, was among them: he had been an early admirer of the revolutionary firebrand Giuseppe Mazzini. Like many of his fellow patriots, Lorenzini accepted that the new Italy would have to be a monarchy because of the pivotal contribution made by Vittorio Emanuele's kingdom, which encompassed Piedmont and Sardinia. But as the new state became progressively distanced from the ideals of its founders in the years following Unification, he and many others became disenchanted. Collodi was able to give vent to his disillusion in excoriating articles in publications including the Florence-based regional newspaper *La*

Nazione. But he made his living by working in the administration, and in the late 1870s the government delivered a warning to public servants against openly criticizing the new state and its politics. Many have assumed that it was Collodi's disillusion alone that drove him into the apparently innocent business of writing for children. Cosimo Ceccuti, in an essay in *Carlo Collodi protagonista dell'Unità d'Italia* (2011), argues that the government warning also had an influence. It is hard to resist the conclusion that by putting a king and a block of wood in the same sentence at the start of his book, Collodi was taking a dig at the monarchy presiding over the gradual descent of Italian politics into corrupt and cynical horse-trading. The link between wood and stupidity is at least as strong in Italian as it is in English: *testa di legno*, for example, has much the same meaning as "blockhead."

3. The Italian expression *un legno da catasta*, literally meaning "a log from a stack," also had the meaning of "rascal" in Florentine colloquial usage during Collodi's time. Already, the author is giving his readers a hint of what is to follow.

4. *Mastr'* in the original Italian: a shortening of *mastro* (an antiquated equivalent of *maestro*), a term used for the head of a workshop, which is ironic in this context since mastr'Antonio works on his own. According to Emilio Broglio and Giovan Battista Giorgini's dictionary of Florentine usage, *Novo vocabolario della lingua italiana secondo l'uso di Firenze* (1870–97), *mastro* was used seldom by Collodi's time and, if so, usually humorously.

5. *Maestro* in the original Italian—further evidence of the prevalence of titles in Italy (see page xvii). *Maestro*, like *Mastro*, should have been reserved for the heads of workshops. In Collodi's time, it was also used for the elderly, and according to Broglio and Giorgini (see preceding note), *maestro* was even used for those who had no other title—even for beggars and tramps. Its closest equivalent today would be the equally common, and meaningless, "Mr."

6. This appears to contradict what Mr. Cherry says before and after, that this is just an ordinary piece of firewood. But it may have been a way for Collodi to underline the carpenter's poverty and that of his customers: any old chunk of wood was good enough to make their rudimentary furniture.

7. Not, as in some translations, an ax or hatchet. Though the Italian word *ascia* is sometimes inappropriately used for an ax or

hatchet, its real meaning is "adze." No carpenter would select an ax or hatchet for the delicate task of stripping bark from a piece of wood that was about to be made into an item of furniture. For that, he would use an instrument for dressing or shaping wood—i.e., an adze: similar to an ax but with its cutting edge perpendicular to the handle.

8. The use of wigs, *parrucche,* was common in Italy, as in the rest of Europe, until the end of the eighteenth century (the practice lives on in the modern-day Italian word for a hairdresser, *parrucchiere*). Yet here is Mr. Cherry still wearing a wig, long after they had gone out of fashion. It makes the carpenter a slightly absurd figure, all the more so since he is scratching his wig rather than his head. The wearing of wigs—and, as we shall see later, his friend Geppetto is also a wig fancier—seems to point to the two craftsmen's pretensions to gentility. That not only makes them yet more ridiculous, but shows the importance of the quintessentially Italian concept of *bella figura* (keeping up appearances in all senses of the word), even among the poor.

9. Beans take a long time to cook, so what Mr. Cherry is saying is that the piece of wood would burn slowly and for a long time. Beans are poor people's fare the world over, but slow-boiled beans, traditionally cooked with sage leaves and served with olive oil (*fagioli all'olio*), or nowadays often with tuna as well (*fagioli con tonno*), are a typical Tuscan specialty. The custom, which still exists, was either to put the beans in a pot inside a brick oven that had been used to bake bread so that they cooked over a period of hours while the oven cooled, or to keep them cooking over an open fire as it burned all day to heat the house. The idea was to take maximum advantage of an energy supply in a culture where it was important not to waste anything. An area close to the town of Collodi from which the author of the *Adventures* took his pen name produces a kind of bean, *fagiolo di Sorana,* that has become a foodie favorite. It has a quality logo, a Protected Geographical Indication (PGI), from the European Union.

10. In the original, *corpo,* which means "body" in standard Italian. But in Tuscany *corpo* also means "belly," and in the *Adventures* it is used with both meanings. The word *corpo* is fundamental to Collodi's masterpiece. At this stage, Pinocchio still has no body, yet "he" is conscious of having one. There are echoes of Michelangelo's view that he was liberating his subjects from the marble in which they were trapped, most starkly evident in his "Prisoners" or "Slaves," on display at the Accademia in Florence: four

unfinished works that are visibly emerging from the stone. They previously stood in the Boboli Gardens in Florence.

CHAPTER 2

11. Geppetto is the endearing diminutive of Geppo, which, in turn, is one of the short forms for Giuseppe, the Italian version of Joseph. So here we have a satirist who has created a carpenter who is also a father-to-be and called him Joseph. As we shall see later, notably at the end of chapter 15, this is not the only parallel between Collodi's fairy tale and the narrative of the New Testament.

12. Cornmeal (polenta) had been a staple of the meager diet of peasants in central and northern Italy since the fifteenth century. But *polentina*, or *polendina* in the Tuscan vernacular version, is an even poorer, mushier dish than polenta.

13. Collodi uses the word *burattino*, which means "puppet." But strictly speaking, a puppet is a figure with a cloth body and a wooden or papier-mâché head, which is moved by a hand inside. Pinocchio instead is a marionette, which is a wooden figure with jointed limbs moved from above by means of attached strings. However, at the time Collodi was writing, *burattino* was used more loosely.

14. The phrase used to describe minimally rewarded employment in Italian, *buscarsi un tozzo di pane,* is almost identical to the English "to earn a crust." But Geppetto adds the colorful, and very Italian, touch of a glass of wine to go with it.

15. Daniela Marcheschi, in her authoritative annotated edition of *Le avventure di Pinocchio* (Milan, 1995, 922–23), points out that the use of a piece of wood that talks has a long history as a device in Italian literature. Virgil, Dante, and Ariosto all employed it, and Collodi drew on all three for inspiration. The device was also used by writers in Collodi's literary circle. Nor was it the first time that Collodi himself had deployed a puppet or a piece of wood in a literary work. Among other instances, in 1877, in an article for *La Vedetta. Gazzetta del popolo*, he created a speaking puppet to "mock, on solemn occasions, with its little scornful laugh" the great powers of Europe and call "in a little voice" for reforms.

16. A good example of the inventiveness of colloquial Tuscan. The phrase is *stinchi impresciuttiti*. The second word refers to the

curing of *prosciutto*. Poor Geppetto's shins are being compared to dried-out old ham bones.

17. The Italian word for "good" used here is not *buono*, but *bravo*, which has paradoxical characteristics. It can be used to mean good at doing something, "good-hearted" or "well-behaved." And in Tuscany it can also mean "nice," which seems to be the sense in this context. But *bravo* can also mean the opposite of good: bad. Already, Collodi appears to be hinting at the two sides of Pinocchio's character.

CHAPTER 3

18. The poverty—indeed, wretchedness—of most of the characters in the *Adventures* is one of its salient features. Almost without exception, its human characters lead thankless existences, working hard for modest rewards and haunted by the threat of hunger. But then that is all of a piece with Collodi's social awareness and his championing of the poor in his journalistic writings.

19. Even though most Italians today are unaware of the fact, when the *Adventures* was written, *pinocchio* was the word for a pine nut. But as the word became irrevocably associated with Collodi's fictional puppet, it was replaced by the word *pinolo*, which, in the 1880s, was used only in colloquial Florentine. In Tuscany, someone with a *testa a pinolo* (a "pine-nut head") is brainless: an "airhead." Instead, someone who is stubborn or stupid is said to be as hard as (green) pine cones (*duro come le pigne [verdi]*).

20. Clearly humorous. Nevertheless, as the late Fernando Tempesti observed in his annotated version of the *Adventures*, published in 1993, begging was a highly structured activity in Italy until the Second World War. Each beggar followed a specific route, known as his or her *gita*, asking for alms on the same streets and/or at the same houses on set days of the week or month. So it is not unthinkable that a beggar in a wealthy area might have made more money than some of Collodi's other characters.

21. Collodi introduces his readers to the puppet's magically extending nose early on. But there is no connection with lying until much later, and even then the link remains surprisingly tenuous.

22. Not as tautological in Collodi's day as it might seem today. It was by no means to be taken for granted that a stone floor

would cover the ground in the lowest story of the kinds of houses occupied by poor Italians in the late nineteenth century.

23. Only city and town streets were paved in Collodi's day. Even then, not all were. Clogs enabled country folk to keep their feet dry and clear of the muddy streets of their villages. Today's Italians have little or no memory of farmers wearing clogs. One of the few reminders is the title of Ermanno Olmi's art house classic *L'albero degli zoccoli* (*The Tree of Wooden Clogs*).

24. A member of Italy's semi-military police force, comparable to the French Gendarmerie, which inspired its creation. The Arma dei Carabinieri was originally the police force of the Kingdom of Sardinia, the country, including much of northwestern Italy, that had the most prominent role in Italy's unification. After Unification, the Carabinieri were deployed throughout the country.

CHAPTER 4

25. It would be hard to think of a more appropriate creature to take the part of an insistent provider of unsolicited advice. The crickets' monotonous, repetitive chirping cannot be silenced. In Collodi's time, crickets were seen in a quite negative light. The noise they make at night was regarded as irritating. And in sufficient numbers, they could do serious damage to crops. In Italian, the cricket was associated with some unpleasant concepts. "To go listen to the crickets chirping" was a euphemism for dying. And an incompetent doctor was known as a cricket doctor. In any event, the insect featured prominently in the life of Collodi's native Florence. The Feast of the Ascension, forty days after Easter, was also, for Florentines, the Festa del Grillo, when families went to Le Cascine, the huge park on the north bank of the Arno downstream of the center, to buy a cricket in a cage. Various reasons have been given for this odd festival, which was banned in 1999 to protect the insects, which were becoming increasingly endangered. According to one theory, it began as an attempt to keep down the numbers of crickets in the surrounding countryside. In another version, the Festa del Grillo celebrated a particular moment in the year: the beginning of summer, which coincides with the arrival of the crickets and their chirping.

26. In Italy, the family home was indeed the father's home and remained so until 1975. It was only then that parliament largely

abolished the concept of the father as *capofamiglia* (head of the family) with legal authority over both his children and his wife.

27. Collodi is cueing up one of the central themes of the *Adventures*: that being a donkey at school—playing the jackass—leads to having to work like a donkey afterward, and that the only way to avoid the fate of a donkey is to get an education.

CHAPTER 5

28. Pinocchio's nose grows for the second time, but once again with no link to mendacity. Here, it grows out of disappointment. In Italian, *rimanerci con un palmo di naso* ("to end up with a palm's width of nose") means to be left disappointed, sometimes as a result of trickery—and, indeed, Pinocchio's nose has just grown by four fingers, the exact width of a palm. Here and subsequently Collodi links the magical extension of the puppet's nose to a saying or expression, but in a subtle and oblique way.

29. Except that we have already been told that Pinocchio does not have any ears. See above in chapter 3, when Geppetto tries to grasp them. Pinocchio's ears go on to appear and disappear throughout the book.

30. In the Italian, not the standard *papà*, but *babbo*. Even though *babbo* is used for "dad" in some other parts of central Italy as well as in Tuscany, the word is considered by other Italians to be archetypally and quintessentially Tuscan. More than any other word or phrase in the *Adventures*, this one tells Italian readers that Pinocchio is a Tuscan kid.

31. *A uso uovo da bere* in the original: a popular way of eating eggs in Collodi's day. The eggs were boiled for a short period in their shells. The yolk and egg white could then be sucked out. Alternatively, bread "fingers" could be dipped into the shells. Pellegrino Artusi in *La scienza in cucina e l'arte di mangiar bene*, the bible of Italian cuisine, published in 1891, calls this *uovo a bere*. He recommends that the egg should be cooked for two minutes.

CHAPTER 6

32. Not a button, of course, this being the late nineteenth century, but a device—connected to a real bell, often some distance away inside the house—that rang the bell when pulled.

CHAPTER 7

33. The first occasion on which Pinocchio tells a lie without his nose growing.
34. Once again, Collodi alludes to a saying, but without actually using it. In this case, the expression is *"Che colpa ne ha la gatta?"* ("Is the cat to blame?"), which is used to indicate that the fault belongs to no one but the person being addressed. It can still be heard in the area of Lucca where the author spent a large part of his childhood.
35. In Italian the expression is *"Pazienza!"*: one of those untranslatable terms, like *chic* and *Schadenfreude,* that speak volumes about the characteristics and values of a culture. Literally, it means "Patience!" but it conveys a fatalistic acceptance of the vagaries of life that doubtless arises from Italians' troubled history. In Collodi's day, resignation was regarded unambiguously as a virtue.
36. Despite what Collodi writes in his summary at the beginning of the chapter, it ends without Pinocchio's feet being remade—another example of the minor inconsistencies that litter the *Adventures.* On several occasions, the summaries at the beginnings of chapters do not match the contents. Collodi was an author and journalist of genius, but not one who was unduly preoccupied with getting all the details right.

CHAPTER 8

37. School attendance was made obligatory in the new Kingdom of Italy at its inception in 1861, but only for two years. In 1877, a new education act came into force. Popularly known as the Legge Coppino, after the minister who sponsored its enactment, the law introduced free elementary schooling for five years, of which the first three were compulsory. The following year, funds were allocated for a major program of school building. Even though Michele Coppino's law introduced sanctions for parents who failed to ensure that their children went to school, its implementation in rural areas was uneven. So the question of how to guarantee that children received an education was topical and controversial in Collodi's day. The author himself was a passionate advocate of the idea that all young

Italians should be educated. It is one of the central themes of
the *Adventures*. But in an open letter to Coppino in 1884, titled
"Pane e libri" (Bread and Books), Collodi argued that the state
could expect children to attend school only if it had first provided their families with the means to feed them adequately.

38. In fact, Pinocchio has already had at least one hat, which he
held out in chapter 6 when begging from the irascible little old
man.

39. In the original—"*E i quattrini?*"—Geppetto is using a colloquial term for money that is still in use today. The *quattrino*
was a low-denomination copper coin used in most of the pre-
Unification states. In the old Grand Duchy of Tuscany, it was
worth one-sixtieth of a *lira*. This is the first of several references
by the characters in the story to the coinage of the Grand Duchy,
which was absorbed into the nascent state of Italy in 1859. That
would seem to set the *Adventures* in the days before Unification.
Yet in chapter 3, Pinocchio is nabbed by a Carabiniere, and the
Carabinieri were not deployed outside the Kingdom of Sardinia
until after the proclamation of the state of Italy in 1861. So it is
unclear when exactly the events in the tale are meant to be taking
place—and that may have been deliberate. As already mentioned,
the *Adventures* offers a pretty bleak picture of Italy as a land of
widespread poverty, many of whose inhabitants live on the brink
of starvation. Collodi may have felt it was prudent to introduce
an element of ambiguity with regard to when exactly his story
was meant to be set. Alternatively, he may just have wanted to
add a layer of unreality to his fable.

40. According to the *Vocabolario italiano della lingua parlata*, edited by Giuseppe Rigutini and Pietro Fanfani and published in
1875–76, this type of coat, known as a *casacca*, was no longer
in use. Collodi may be reinforcing the point made above, in the
previous note, or stressing that the bewigged Geppetto is reduced to wearing clothes that not only are patched and worn,
but also have long since gone out of fashion.

CHAPTER 9

41. The *soldo* (plural, *soldi*) was another low-denomination copper
coin in the currency of the pre-Unification Grand Duchy of
Tuscany. It was worth three *quattrini* (see note 39) or a twentieth of a *lira*.

CHAPTER 10

42. When, in 1999, the Tuscan comic actor Roberto Benigni won the Oscar for Best Actor for his role in *La vita è bella* (*Life Is Beautiful*), he astonished his fellow nominees and assembled Hollywood luminaries by setting out for the stage by walking on the backs of the seats in front of him. It is hard to resist the conclusion that Benigni, a great admirer of Collodi's fable, who was born not far from Florence, was inspired to do so by Pinocchio. The puppet and his antics would have been at the forefront in his mind at the time, since he had already conceived the idea of directing his own movie version of Collodi's tale. Announced the following year, Benigni's *Pinocchio* was released in 2002, with Benigni playing the part of the puppet. He had also been involved with Federico Fellini in an earlier project to turn the *Adventures* into a movie. Sadly, the film was never made.

43. An odd metaphor perhaps for today's readers, but a reminder that people in Collodi's day were writing with thick ink and low-quality pens, so a scribble could indeed look like a scraggly beard.

44. The reference here is to the opening of a woodfire oven, like those used to make pizza. When the fire inside is not lit, the opening is large, black, and, to a child, potentially frightening.

45. Roasting a whole ram for one person's dinner was as implausible in Collodi's day as it would be today. But it figures in a famous French fairy tale that Collodi translated, Charles Perrault's "Le Petit Poucet," published in 1697 and known in English since the early nineteenth century as "Hop-o'-My-Thumb." In "Le Petit Poucet," it is an ogre living in the woods who consumes an entire sheep for his dinner—and, as with the ram roasted by the ogreish puppeteer, the animal is less than fully cooked.

CHAPTER 11

46. A question that may seem odd to today's readers, but which would not have seemed out of place to those for whom Collodi was writing. Even among those who survived infancy, the mortality rate in late nineteenth-century Italy was extremely high.

So it was far from unusual for children to have only one parent, or none. In 1883, the year in which the *Adventures* was published, the median age of death among Italians over the age of five was 54.8 for women and 56.0 for men. Source: ISTAT.

47. In Italian, *giandarmi*, a term for Carabinieri that was obsolete by the time the *Adventures* was published—a further example of Collodi's blurring of time frames.

CHAPTER 12

48. The *zecchino* (plural, *zecchini*) was originally a Venetian coin that subsequently became legal tender in other Italian states including Tuscany. By Collodi's time, it was no longer in use, so the mention of *zecchini* enhances the fairy-tale atmosphere of his story. *Zecchini* were anything but "miserable" in their day. According to Eupremio Montenegro's *Manuale del collezionista di monete italiane* (29th ed., Turin, 2008), in Tuscany during the reign of Leopoldo II (1824–59), a *zecchino* was worth 2,000 *quattrini*. In chapter 9, Pinocchio sells his spelling book for the price of a ticket to the puppet theater: four *soldi*, the equivalent of twelve *quattrini*. So, to have earned five *zecchini*, Fire-eater would need to have sold well over eight hundred tickets. He has given Pinocchio, or rather Geppetto, a very considerable sum of money. No wonder the Fox and Cat are so eager to get their hands on it.

49. In the original, the land of the Barbagianni, or barn owls. As in many cultures, in Italy, these birds of prey are regarded as spooky. But the word *barbagianni*, which is the same in the singular as in the plural, is also used used to mean "dupe" or "sucker."

50. Pinocchio is subtly disowning responsibility for his own misbehavior. And not for the last time. Again and again in the pages that follow, he starts by blaming himself for his misfortune only to come around to attributing it to factors beyond his control.

51. It seems there really was a "Field of Miracles" where gold coins multiplied. It was outside Colonnata, now a district of Florence, on the grounds of a noble mansion, the Villa Gerini. It was there that a gardener found two baskets buried in the ground containing 100 gold florins. But as Nicola Rilli recounts in *Pinocchio in casa sua*, published in 1973, the number of coins that had been discovered increased in the retelling until they became several thousand. Rilli, a local historian who

conducted dozens of interviews in an area on the northwestern outskirts of Florence, identified a number of people and places that Collodi appeared to have used as inspiration in writing the *Adventures*. The area, north of Amerigo Vespucci airport, takes in several districts that in the late nineteenth century were towns in their own right. They include Colonnata, Peretola, and, most important, Castello.

52. The Fox is echoing the point made by the Talking Cricket in chapter 4: that, if you have no education, people will make a fool of you. Pinocchio cannot do any sort of calculation because he has not gone to school. The Fox's arithmetic is correct, but he could have made up any mathematical nonsense he liked and the puppet would have been unable to challenge him.

CHAPTER 13

53. The Red Crayfish—Il Gambero Rosso in the original—has been used as the name of many an Italian restaurant. The most renowned was at San Vincenzo on the Tuscan coast, where, for almost thirty years, the chef was Fulvio Pierangelini. Several times judged Italy's best restaurant, Il Gambero Rosso closed its doors in 2009, and subsequently reopened, but only to close again in 2012. *Gambero Rosso* is also the name of a leading Italian gastronomic periodical, which publishes several restaurant guides and has a satellite TV channel of its own. Nicola Rilli, in *Pinocchio in casa sua*, identifies the original as an *osteria* in Colonnata, where the specialty was river crayfish.

54. Foxes in Italian are, by default, grammatically feminine, and Collodi does not at any point make it clear that his fox is a male. The notion that the Fox, whom we first encounter leaning for support on the Cat, might be a vixen was taken up in a self-published translation of the *Adventures*, that by Gloria Italiano, the wife of the founder of the Fondazione Nazionale Carlo Collodi. The only set of illustrations that Collodi approved in his lifetime, those by Enrico Mazzanti, shows the two villains as animals, with no anthropomorphic characteristics. But politicians were often described or depicted as foxes in the satirical journals to which Collodi contributed. In Italy, the phrase *il Gatto e la Volpe*, the Cat and the Fox, has become a common expression to describe two characters of dubious intentions who are inseparable and work together to rip off the gullible.

55. In Italian, *cibreo*: a traditional Florentine culinary specialty. It did not in fact contain lizards, but it nevertheless included some ingredients that would be considered unusual today, such as chicken crests and testicles. It was said to have been a favorite dish of the Florentine-born Caterina de' Medici, who ruled France as queen consort from 1547 to 1559. Cibreo is the name of one of Florence's most famous restaurants.

56. In Collodi's time, as in many Italian towns and cities today, the time could be told by the tolling of a bell, usually on a nearby church.

CHAPTER 14

57. This is the second time that Pinocchio has been caught by the nose. The first time was in chapter 3, when he was grabbed by the brave Carabiniere, and Collodi remarked then that the nose seemed to have been made for the purpose. It has also grown twice, the first time when he was being made and the second as a result of disappointment. So Collodi at this stage in his narrative regarded Pinocchio's nose as a multifunctional literary instrument. But lie detection was still not among its various functions.

58. Pinocchio's choice of tree could not be more appropriate, remembering that, at the time Collodi was writing, Pinocchio meant "pine nut." See note 19.

CHAPTER 15

59. *Turchino* in the original, frequently mistranslated as "turquoise." It means dark blue. Since the nineteenth century, *turchino* has gradually been supplanted by the word *blu*, an import that began life as the French *bleu*. Mid- and light blue are *azzurro* and *celeste*, respectively. Turquoise is *turchese*.

60. It is tempting to speculate on whether, in this dreamlike and terrifying episode, Collodi is recalling traumatic images from his childhood. Of his nine siblings, five died before reaching the age of seven. Of these, the longest-lived, Marianna Seconda, was six years younger than Carlo. Perhaps his memories of her death at age six are to be found in this profoundly eerie passage. His description of the little girl could be that of a corpse at a wake.

61. In Italian, to be made of wood means to be stubborn. The phrase is *essere duro come il legno*. Here, Pinocchio is described as being not just made of wood but made of hard wood—a fact that is referred to several times in the book.

62. There is good reason to believe that Collodi had in mind an actual tree when he wrote about the hanging of Pinocchio. According to Gian Luigi Corinto and Fabio Norcini in *Pinocchio Fiorentino: Mali antichi e antichi rimedi* (2020), the tree was in Castello, then a small town and now a suburb of Florence where Collodi spent time because his brother Paolo lived there for part of the year in a mansion, Villa Il Bel Riposo. The tree was known to locals as La Quercia Grande, the Big Oak. It had a sinister reputation in the neighborhood: it was widely believed that witches gathered around it at night.

63. The parallels with the final phase of Jesus's crucifixion are striking. "And at the ninth hour Jesus cried with a loud voice, '*Eloi Eloi lema sabachthani?*' which means, 'My God, my God, why have you forsaken me?'" (Mark 15:34). Equally striking is that Pinocchio calls for the help of his "father," Geppetto, using the familiar form of "you," *tu*. Previously, he has always addressed the carpenter using *voi*. In the Italian translation of the invocation above, Jesus also uses *tu*.

64. This is the supremely grim fate that Collodi originally intended for Pinocchio: it was how he chose to end the run of installments published in the *Giornale per i bambini* between July and October. Only after an outcry from his readers was he persuaded to continue the story on an altogether brighter note in a second run of installments early the following year.

65. Is Collodi also telling his young readers not to be too attached to money? Pinocchio dies because he dodges school, will not listen to advice from those who are more experienced than he is, but also because he believes in quick money—and is even prepared to die for it.

CHAPTER 16

66. She may have been inspired by a real person. An article published in 1956 (R. Gazzaniga, "Vive in un paese presso Firenze la Fata di Pinocchio dai capelli turchini," *Il Giornale del Mattino*, April 10, 1956, 3) identified her as Giovanna Ragionieri, who had been born in 1868. Though by then in her late eighties, and

known by her married name of Giovanna Giannini, Ragionieri still had the strikingly blue eyes that had marked her out as a child. Her father was the gardener at Villa Il Bel Riposo in Castello (see note 62), and as a girl of twelve, she went to work there herself as a housemaid. By her own account in subsequent interviews, Collodi told her that he was going to put her into his story. Her version of events was widely accepted in Italy to the extent that she became something of a celebrity before her death in 1962. She received letters from children all over the country and was visited by at least one famous show business personality. Ragionieri was thirteen years old when Collodi began writing the *Adventures* and fifteen when he finished. That offers a possible explanation of why he gave the character in the *Adventures* a double identity, first as a little girl and then as a Fairy who later takes the form of a grown woman. In nineteenth-century Italy, a fifteen-year-old was considered to be on the brink of adulthood. If Giovanna Ragionieri were the model for the most prominent female character in the *Adventures*, it could also explain another idiosyncrasy of the story, which is that whereas the Little Girl lives in a small house in the woods when Pinocchio is hanged, she appears to occupy a mansion, complete with stables and carriages, after becoming a Fairy in the present chapter. Collodi knew Giovanna both in the context of her modest family home and as a servant at the much grander Villa Il Bel Riposo. According to Corinto and Norcini in *Pinocchio Fiorentino* (see note 62), the Ragionieris' home was at the edge of a wood, three hundred feet or so from the Villa Il Bel Riposo. The Quercia Grande (see note 62) was in the middle of the wood and could be seen from both their cottage and the mansion.

67. The name of a character in Ludovico Ariosto's sixteenth-century epic poem *Orlando furioso,* echoes of which recur throughout the book. Medoro is a strikingly handsome Muslim warrior with whom Angelica, a pagan princess, falls in love. Their liaison, across sectarian boundaries, provided inspiration for Giovanni Battista Tiepolo and became a popular subject for Romantic painters, composers, and writers. Medoro was also the name of a dog who became internationally renowned during the July Revolution of 1830 in Paris. He carried his master's rifle and ammunition and refused for days on end to abandon his master's grave after the man had been killed and buried in the courtyard of the Louvre.

68. This peculiar description has puzzled literary critics ever since the publication of the *Adventures*. Some translators have left it out altogether. But the consensus among Italian scholars of Collodi is that he is alluding to the glistening painted surface of the carriage—or maybe even to its being invisible. An alternative explanation is that, having turned his children's story into something that is much more of a fairy tale, Collodi is using the freedom that affords him to deploy a beautiful metaphor that would do justice to a work of magical realism.

69. Collodi may well have drawn his inspiration for this passage from the exploits of the American showman P. T. Barnum and his star human attraction, Charles Stratton (1838–83), who never grew to a height of more than three feet and who appeared under the name of General Tom Thumb. Daniela Marcheschi writes that on one of his tours of Europe, "Tom Thumb was lionized by the crowds and exalted by the newspapers, especially in Florence." Contemporary prints show the "General" riding in a tiny carriage, drawn by minute horses and driven by a boy wearing a wig and tricorn hat.

CHAPTER 17

70. The first indication that the transformation of the Little Girl into a fairy is accompanied by a change in her nature and demeanor. The ethereal child of the first part abruptly becomes a solicitous mother figure while nevertheless remaining a little girl. She calls the doctors, listens to what they have to say, and puts her hand on Pinocchio's forehead to judge his temperature in just the way a real mother might.

71. In the Italian original, the medicine is a *purgativo*, or laxative. Such remedies were popular in the nineteenth century as a way to purify the body. The concept went out of fashion until revived under a new guise in recent years as detoxification. The white powder dissolved by the Fairy is most probably what is known in Italy as *sale inglese* (Epsom salt), magnesium sulfate.

72. An example of the fairy-tale paraphernalia that Collodi introduced into his story when he returned to it in the second run of installments. The golden sugar bowl is all of a piece with the Fairy's improbably furnished carriage, Medoro's livery, and mother-of-pearl bedroom walls.

73. At one level, this is simply humorous. Pinocchio is scared by, of all creatures, rabbits—animals universally symbolizing timidity. But in a book written by a Florentine, the undertaker rabbits have a significance that any Tuscan would recognize instantly: in their floppy, pointed black hoods and long black robes that reach to the ground, the members of the elite Venerabile Arci-confraternita della Misericordia di Firenze look like nothing so much as giant black rabbits. Founded in 1244, the Misericordia claims to be the world's oldest private voluntary association. Its members' garb, which has been black since 1495, was designed to hide the identity of its volunteers so that they would give their services to the community without expecting any kind of praise or reward. The members of the fraternity could be seen in the streets of Florence wearing their imposing, if somewhat creepy, garb until quite recently. And it is still worn for ceremonial purposes. The special mission of the Misericordia has always been to help the sick, and in earlier times its members took on the un-enviable task of carrying away the dead bodies of plague victims for burial. Collodi may well have been inspired to put black rabbits in the *Adventures* after they were used in a satirical review, *Rigoletto*, to lampoon Bettino Ricasoli, the Tuscan landowner and nobleman who succeeded Count Cavour to become Italy's second prime minister. Collodi had originally been an enthusiastic supporter of Ricasoli but had become disillusioned with him by the mid-1870s because of the politician's incapacity and maybe unwillingness to solve the underlying problems of the nascent Kingdom of Italy. As a political satirist himself, Collodi would almost certainly have been an avid reader of *Rigoletto,* and as a critic of Ricasoli he would no doubt have been amused by the way in which the rabbits were depicted: following the statesman and carrying the instruments needed to give him an enema.

74. As pointed out in the Note on the Translation, while the Fairy was simply a child, Pinocchio addressed her using *tu,* the informal form of "you." But now that she has the trappings of an adult and the status of a thousand-year-old Fairy, he switches to *voi,* which in Collodi's day was one of two formal forms, known in Italian as *pronomi di cortesia* (courtesy pronouns). *Voi* was for more familiar contexts and was used by children to show respect for their parents and by servants to show respect for the children of the family they were serving. But in less

intimate situations, *lei* would have been expected. Pinocchio always uses *voi* when addressing his "father," Geppetto.

75. This has become far and away Pinocchio's most celebrated characteristic: the propensity of his nose to grow whenever he tells a lie. Yet it is not introduced until here, in the second run of installments. Had Pinocchio's adventures ended at the point at which Collodi originally intended, there would have been no association between the puppet and lying.

76. Often translated in previous editions as "a couple of inches." But the original is unequivocal: *due dita* (two fingers), as when measuring out spirits. So at first Pinocchio's nose grows quite modestly, almost as if it were a warning for him to reconsider. Pinocchio being Pinocchio, he of course ignores the hint and digs himself in deeper.

77. *Le bugie hanno le gambe corte*, or "Lies have short legs," is an Italian proverb. It means that lies can go only so far, but no further, before being unmasked. However, the Fairy's reference to lies with long noses is not reflected in any widely known popular saying. The closest link is perhaps with the phrase *la bugia ti corre su per il naso,* which means that a lie can be detected on your face as it runs up on your nose to your forehead. There are other links between lies and noses in the Tuscan oral tradition, but nothing that refers to the length of the nose. So it would seem that the credit for the book's most renowned flight of fantasy belongs entirely to Collodi. What is not entirely clear is what the Fairy means when she distinguishes lies with short legs from those with long noses. One possible explanation is that lies with long noses are meant to be those that are instantly recognizable—just like long noses.

CHAPTER 18

78. An example of Collodi's inversion of literary convention. As in other cultures, the wolf in Italy was regarded until very recently as a perilous animal. The assumption that wolves are only too ready to kill and eat human beings crops up in any number of fairy tales, most famously "Little Red Riding Hood," which Collodi had translated into Italian from French. The story appears in *I racconti delle fate* (1876). Yet here is Collodi turning the only wolf in his story into a creature asking for help. And what is more, from two animals that could be its prey.

79. *Acchiappa-citrulli* in the original, from *acchiappare* ("catch")
and the plural of *citrullo*, a variant of *cetriolo* ("cucumber"),
used figuratively to mean a stupid or gullible person. Several
commentators have speculated that Collodi had in mind his native Florence. In 1865, after the declaration of the new state of
Italy, but before the process of unification was complete, Florence was made the capital. On the assumption that it would remain the capital indefinitely, ambitious projects of urban
renewal were undertaken to adapt the city to its new role. Min-
istries and other government departments were set up in Florence and large numbers of state employees flooded into the city.
But in 1870 Italian troops captured Rome, and the following
year Rome became the capital. Florence, and many Florentines,
never received the expected return on their investments. The
city was left heavily indebted and for many years afterward its
inhabitants had to pay increased taxes to repay its borrowings.
Not only were they poorer, but many were no doubt left with a
feeling that they had been taken for a ride.

80. Is that because they are in the Land of the Barn Owls? Collodi
appears to be maintaining the ambiguity of the word *barbagianni* (see note 49).

CHAPTER 19

81. A sweet liquor that has been produced in Italy since at least the
sixteenth century, made by mixing alcohol, water, and sugar.
Though rosewater is used to flavor some, but by no means all,
kinds of rosolio, the name has nothing to do with roses. The
most commonly accepted etymology has it that the word is a
corruption of Latin *ros solis* ("dew of the sun"). Aniseed, mint,
coffee, and citrus fruits are all used to flavor different varieties of
rosolio.

82. A sweet, spicy, and luridly scarlet-colored liqueur. In addition
to being an after-dinner drink, alkermes is used for soaking the
sponge cake or ladyfingers that go into making *zuppa inglese,* a
dessert similar to Britain's trifle. In Italian the spelling is *al-
chermes*. The word derives from Arabic *kirmiz*, the name of the
insect originally used to produce the liqueur's distinct color.

83. The *Galateo overo de' costumi*, a guide to social etiquette written by Giovanni Della Casa (1503–56) and first published in
1558. It became so well known that Italians took to using *il*

Galateo as a synonym for socially acceptable behavior, as in this instance.

84. *Barbagianni,* or "barn owls," in the original. See note 49.

85. A fine example of the intricacy and subtlety that disappears in translation. The expression is *"dolce di sale,"* which literally means "sweet of salt." In Italian, *dolce* can be used to denote a lack of salt, as in *acqua dolce* (fresh water), or a low content of salt, as in *prosciutto dolce* (ham that is cured with less salt than other types). *Sale,* salt, is often used to symbolize intelligence: the word *sciocco,* for example, means both "not salty" and "stupid." Another Italian expression is *avere sale nella zucca* ("to have salt in your pumpkin"), in which the pumpkin represents the head. It is thus no coincidence that Collodi goes on to use pumpkins as an example of what you can successfully plant in a field. Artful linkages such as these are a common feature of Collodi's writing.

CHAPTER 20

86. Note the quotation marks. This is Collodi at his most original and inventive—almost surrealistic. The question does not come from the narrator (who answers it in the following paragraph), but from an unexplained voice speaking from outside the book, presumably one of the little readers the narrator addresses at the very beginning of chapter 1 and to whom he turns now and then throughout the story.

CHAPTER 21

87. Fireflies are a common nighttime sight in the Tuscan countryside in early summer. This is consistent with several months having passed since Geppetto was shivering in his shirtsleeves and there was snow on the ground at the end of chapter 8. See also note 105.

88. A sign of what has already been hinted at in chapter 17 when Pinocchio's nose grows for the first time when he tells a lie—that Collodi's story becomes increasingly moralizing in the second run of installments.

89. Even today, the attitude of older farmers in southern Europe ranges from unsentimental to downright cruel. Dogs for hunt-

ing are often kept penned up in miserable conditions. And when they outlive their usefulness, it is quite normal for them to be shot or abandoned. Younger farmers are gradually adopting more humane practices, and there has been a noticeable improvement in the treatment of farmyard guard dogs like Melampus. Until the end of the twentieth century, they were rarely given enough to eat and spent their lives on the end of a chain.

CHAPTER 22

90. The name is ironic. Melampus in Greek mythology was a soothsayer who could understand the language of animals. Collodi also used the name Melampus for a large watchdog in "L'omino anticipato," a short story that later appeared in an anthology, *Storie allegre,* published in 1887, and in a school textbook, *Libro di letture per la terza classe elementare secondo gli ultimi programmi*, in 1889.

91. Typically, peasant farmers in Tuscany, as in many other parts of Italy, had their living quarters on the upper floor of their two-story farmhouses, while the lower floor was used to stable their animals. This arrangement helped keep the living quarters above freezing during the often harsh Tuscan winter.

CHAPTER 23

92. Collodi seems to be unable to make up his mind whether she is a little girl, as she was in chapter 15, or the fairy of chapter 17.

93. See note 66.

94. This is the second time the blue-haired Little Girl/Fairy has died. As already noted, Collodi lost several of his sisters in childhood. Could the loss of his sisters be why he had such difficulty letting his fictional Little Girl die? He has already resurrected her once and turned her into the Fairy. As will be seen later, he resurrects the Fairy too. And finally he seems to bring her back from the brink of death in the last chapter.

95. Once again, we get an insight into Collodi's understanding of child psychology. Pinocchio's innate egocentricity surfaces even in the midst of his abject grief.

96. *Colombo* in the original, not *piccione*. The latter is used normally to describe pigeons in general. *Colombo,* on the other

hand, is used for doves, but also for carrier pigeons. The latter is seemingly what Collodi is referring to here. And the pigeon does indeed carry Pinocchio all night long. Once again, there are echoes of Ariosto. The hippogriff, a winged horse, is used to transport several of the characters in *Orlando furioso*.

97. *Per carità* in the original, which literally means "For [the sake of] charity." It is notable that Collodi does not use the expression in Italian for "For Heaven's sake." But then, like many of the other leading figures in the Risorgimento, he was secular. Using *"Per carità,"* as he does repeatedly in the *Adventures,* would fit with his outlook on life, laying greater stress, as it does, on human kindness than on consideration for the divine.

98. In the 1880s, for people in Europe, "the world" was to a large extent the Old World. The New World was a very distant place indeed, that in a fairy tale sounded like another planet. In the Italian collective imagination of Collodi's time, leaving for the New World involved a very long journey even for the passengers to embark on the ship that would carry them across the ocean. In the period from Italian Unification to the outbreak of World War I, at least nine million Italians emigrated permanently and perhaps another five million temporarily. But although it is widely assumed, particularly in the United States, that the overwhelming majority of migrants came from Italy's poverty-stricken south, that became true only after the turn of the twentieth century. Before that, most Italian emigrants were from the center or north of the new state, including from Tuscany.

99. In the original, *"Più di mille chilometri"* ("More than a thousand kilometers"). But Collodi sometimes uses *mille* (a thousand) in the way the Bible uses "forty," to mean a great number not intended to be taken literally. A thousand kilometers would, in fact, take Tuscans to the toe of Italy and perhaps to Sicily. But they would have been more likely to embark for the New World in Genoa, which is only about 225 kilometers (140 miles) from Florence.

100. Not for nothing is another name for them in English Poor Man's Peas.

101. In Italian, the verb is *brontolare* (to grumble). Especially in Italian, it would never be associated with the act of praying. What Collodi is apparently trying to convey here is that the fishermen have seen such terrible loss of life at sea that they have ceased to have faith in a benign God. Such is the extent of their resignation

that they don't even try to save either Geppetto or Pinocchio. Collodi appears to have felt that this was an important point, because he repeats exactly the same words just a few lines below. He is alluding to something to which other authors devoted entire books. One example is Giovanni Verga's *I Malavoglia*, which came out in 1881, the same year Collodi began publishing Pinocchio's story in the *Giornale per i bambini*. *I Malavoglia* was the inspiration for Luchino Visconti's 1948 movie *La terra trema*.

CHAPTER 24

102. In the original, the hyper-Italian *"Mamma mia!"*—which, it should be noted, does not have for Italians the same comic ring that it has for speakers of English.

103. Collodi merely calls it *"il paese delle Api industriose"*: the town of the Busy Bees.

104. The woman appears to be referring to a type of sweet that was popular in Collodi's day. It was hollow and had to be filled with rosolio (see note 81) immediately before it was consumed. In Tuscany, it was called *mangia e bevi* (eat and drink).

105. This curious formulation—in Italian too you would normally write "for months"—may have a perfectly good explanation in the context of the story. Bear in mind that Pinocchio was in jail, and presumably not very well fed, for four months. If another month is allowed for his various adventures before and after prison, it comes to a total of five. As can be seen in other parts of the book, Collodi could be remarkably slapdash, yet also strikingly precise.

CHAPTER 25

106. Yet, as Collodi has just written in the previous chapter, only five months have gone by. His time distortion is among the characteristics of the *Adventures* that give it its oneiric quality. This is the point at which the Blue-haired Fairy's new role as a mother figure (see note 70) becomes explicit. It has been observed that blue is the color most often associated with the Virgin Mary, the ultimate mother figure for Catholics, and it is

tempting to speculate that Collodi was, perhaps unconsciously, transforming his fairy into a Madonna.

107. Suddenly, Pinocchio's identity as a puppet takes on the power of metaphor. Until now, it has been possible to think of him more or less as a naughty little boy. But now his being a marionette becomes central to the story—and to the message, of the importance of education, that Collodi is using the story to convey. If you don't study and make a contribution to society, you will forever remain a puppet. You will never grow. And, as the story goes on to relate, your life will be blighted.

108. Instead of using the verb "to be," *essere*, Pinocchio here uses *fare*, which usually means "to do" or "to make." *Essere* is existential, whereas *fare* is used in the sense of playing a role. It signals that Pinocchio feels in his heart that it is not his role to be a puppet forever; that he is, to some extent, playing a part.

109. Not "boy." But then "man" (*uomo*) in Italian has the same ambiguity as in English. It can mean "human being" as well as "grown male." Collodi is anticipating Pinocchio's later development—his joining the human race and becoming a responsible young adult.

CHAPTER 26

110. In the original, Collodi specifies that the school is *comunale*, which means it was run by the local authority and would have offered basic education for free. See note 37.

111. In a memoir titled "Quand'ero ragazzo!," published in 1887 in *Storie allegre* (see note 90), Collodi recounted how he played a similar prank on one of his schoolmates, drawing on his pants while he was asleep. Indeed, there are reasons for believing that Collodi modeled Pinocchio, at least to some extent, on his younger self. In *Collodi e Pinocchio* (1954), his nephew Paolo Lorenzini, using the pseudonym "Collodi Nipote," quoted his father, the author's brother, as having told him that as a boy Collodi often escaped from the family home to go running around in the fields with his friends. The author himself wrote that, between the ages of eleven and twelve, he went from being the most unruly boy in his class to being a model pupil.

112. Collodi is returning to the theme that he has already introduced (see note 27) and that will become crucially important as the story progresses: that failing to apply oneself at school—being a

"donkey"—leads inexorably to a life that is little better than that of a real donkey.

CHAPTER 27

113. These are all schoolbooks that were in use at the time. They appeared in the catalogue released by the Libreria Editrice Felice Paggi, the Florentine firm that published Collodi's school texts, two of which, *Giannettino* and *Minuzzolo*, get hurled at Pinocchio. Paggi also published the first edition of *The Adventures of Pinocchio* in 1883. *Giannettino* and *Minuzzolo* were highly successful. *Giannettino* was a runaway bestseller and earned Collodi a knighthood as a Cavaliere della Corona d'Italia. However, Filippo Canali, in *Carlo "Collodi" Lorenzini: Un comunicatore nel XIX secolo* (2016), writes that some people deemed the books to be excessively entertaining. One critic wrote that they were "too joyful to be useful for teaching purposes."

114. Once again, *mamma mia!*

115. *Palio*, in the original: the word used for a locally and, in earlier times, informally organized horse race. By far the most famous is the twice-yearly *palio* held in the precipitously inclined main square of Siena, the Piazza del Campo.

CHAPTER 28

116. Another dog with an exalted name, although this one is more appropriate than either Medoro or Melampus. Alidoro means "golden wings." It is also the name of one of the leading characters in Bernardo Tasso's sixteenth-century epic poem *L'Amadigi* and that of the tutor to Don Ramiro, the prince of Salerno, in Rossini's *La Cenerentola*, first performed in 1810.

CHAPTER 29

117. Another play on words: to be fried in Italian also means to be done for.

118. Pinocchio has just told another lie, but this time his nose has not grown.

119. Pinocchio lies for the third time to the little old man, but for the second time his nose does not grow. It is as if Collodi were drawing a distinction between unacceptable lies (Pinocchio claiming that he is a model of good behavior) and acceptable lies, motivated by embarrassment.

120. Fernando Tempesti speculates that Collodi drew his inspiration for this episode from *Ricordi di Roma* by Louis Michel James Lacour-Delatre, which was published in 1870. It includes a story relating to the Irish volunteers who came to defend the pope and the Papal State during the upheavals that preceded Italy's unification. Lacour-Delatre, who was hostile to the papacy, claimed that, having been assured they would be provided with uniforms in Rome, the Irish "left all their clothes in Ireland and arrived wearing potato sacks with one hole for the neck and two for the arms."

121. The same number of stories as the Villa Il Bel Riposo (see note 62): further support for the theory that Collodi used it as his model for the Fairy's home when it is depicted as a mansion. See note 66.

122. Once again, Pinocchio neatly disowns responsibility for his own recklessness, dismissing the consequence as a *disgrazia*, an unfortunate occurrence; an accident or mishap.

123. In Collodi's day, this would have been a sumptuous breakfast, if only because of the liberal use of butter, a rarity in nineteenth-century Tuscany. *Caffè e latte* has since come to be known in Italian as *caffellatte*. It is chiefly drunk at home with breakfast; seldom in a bar. The same appears to have been true of Collodi's time, because there is no mention of the drink on any bill of fare in Italy until the twentieth century. Unlike the "caffè latte" or "latte" offered to customers in cafés outside Italy, the Italian original has little or no milk foam.

124. See note 107.

CHAPTER 30

125. The idea that butter is an alien ingredient and olive oil the only truly Italian fat is a myth, encouraged by the popularization of the "Mediterranean diet." Alberto Capatti and Massimo Montanari, in their landmark history of Italian cuisine, *La cucina italiana: Storia di una cultura* (1999), tell a more complicated story: starting in the late fifteenth century, butter was in fact

used on the peninsula, and not just in the north. But like olive oil, it was expensive and, unlike olive oil, it was difficult to keep in hot weather, so its use tended to be restricted to wealthier households. Poor Italians were more likely to rely on lard. Tuscany seems to have been among the areas in which butter made fewest inroads. Certainly, very few Tuscan recipes call for its use.

126. In Collodi's account of his childhood in *Storie allegre* (see note 111), he mentioned that in Italy at that time there was no school on Thursdays. Children did attend school on Saturdays, as many still do. He wryly remarked that there was "barely one [Thursday] a week!" and it was a godsend that Sundays came around every seven days.

127. We have been told in chapter 29 that Pinocchio has just passed his end-of-school exams and now Lampwick is suggesting that the puppet is either about to enter middle school or already there. That would make Pinocchio about eleven or twelve years old, the same age as the young Collodi of *Storie allegre* (see note 111): additional support for the theory that Pinocchio was Collodi's alter ego.

CHAPTER 31

128. A fashion in Collodi's day. In his earlier work *Minuzzolo*, published in 1877, Collodi described the popularity of ankle boots made of white *vacchetta*, a kind of leather that is a Tuscan specialty. Mentioning them serves two purposes. It helps Collodi maintain a rapport with his young readers in much the same way that an author in the twenty-first century might put sneakers on one of his characters. But it also enables him to intimate that perhaps the donkeys are not quite what they seem.

129. This otherwise apparently routine simile would have had a more profound resonance in the Italy of the 1880s. Daniela Marcheschi points out that *burro* was in those days used colloquially to signify flattery and exaggerated praise. That meaning has since been lost from Italian, though it has an echo in the English phrase "to butter up."

130. "Kids, as soon as they saw him, fell in love with him." The Little Man in turn addresses Lampwick as "my handsome boy . . . my sweet boy" and Pinocchio as "my love." Is Collodi hinting at something that would doubtless have been unprintable in the

1880s? Is he using his story to warn his young readers that men who seem delightful and want to take them on a journey are very possibly predatory pedophiles? Fernando Tempesti, one of Italy's foremost commentators on the *Adventures*, dismissed the notion as a modern interpretation. But the evidence is nevertheless striking.

131. This is behavior worthy of a *mafioso,* and Collodi may indeed have viewed the Little Man in that light. Italians outside Sicily were just beginning to learn about the Mafia when Pinocchio's creator was writing. In Giovanni Verga's short story about rural Sicily, "Cavalleria rusticana," published in 1880—the inspiration for Pietro Mascagni's opera of the same name—Turiddu, a young villager, bites the ear of his enemy to signal that they must duel to the death. It has long been believed that ear-biting has a symbolic significance in the organization.

132. From "Te Voglio Bene Assaje," a smash hit written in Naples in 1839. The lyrics of the song were written by an optician, Raffaele Sacco. The music was of unknown provenance, but may have been written by Donizetti. Before the advent of recordings, the success of a song was measured by the sales of its sheet music. In an age when the most popular songs rarely sold more than 10,000 copies, "Te Voglio Bene Assaje" sold 180,000. Contemporary accounts speak of the maddeningly catchy tune being hummed or whistled on every street corner in Naples—to the extent that some people were said to have fled the city just to get away from it—and in 1840 the authorities banned the Neapolitans from singing or playing it outdoors, for fear that it would compromise the solemnity of religious processions. It can even occasionally be heard today. Sacco's optician's store, the oldest in Italy, is still in business.

133. Part of a proverb from Parma that intimates that whatever someone is complaining about is of little importance.

134. A game dating back to Roman times, when it was known as *nuces castellatae* or *ludus castellorum,* in which players formed a base of three walnuts and then attempted to pitch or drop a fourth so that it would come to rest on the others without causing the base to disintegrate.

135. Another popular game, played with flat stones or tiles. It has several variants.

136. The plural is significant. This was a period in which, because of the increased requirement for the education of children in the

1877 Legge Coppino (see note 37), many new schools were being built.

137. Collodi again contradicts the chapter summary: by the end of this chapter, Pinocchio has not yet become a donkey, nor has the reader even been told that the puppet's ears have become donkey's ears. In fact, Collodi has ruined the cliffhanger ending of his chapter.

CHAPTER 32

138. *Spazzole di padule*, made from the heads of swamp reeds (often *Arundo donax*), were once common in Tuscan households, and because they were soft—like donkeys' ears—they could be used for delicate cleaning, such as the dusting of furniture and paintings in the houses of the wealthy, or the brushing out of the *madia*, the chest used for storing bread. The area between Florence and the town of Collodi still has extensive areas of swampy terrain, though less than in the late nineteenth century.

139. An animal almost identical to a groundhog or woodchuck. Marmots hibernate underground, and in Italian the word for a marmot, *marmotta*, is also used for someone who is lazy and likes to sleep a lot: a "couch potato." So it is perfectly appropriate for a marmot to be found living in Playland.

140. Parmesan cheese is made in big, round "wheels" wider than they are tall. A mouse that found itself in one would be fortunate indeed: Parmesan is not only delicious, but also extremely costly. Italians are likely to come across a wheel of Parmesan only in a delicatessen or at a grand reception.

141. Once again, Pinocchio tells a lie and his nose remains the same. But once again, he is lying out of embarrassment, and that, Collodi seems to suggest, is permissible.

142. Yet another lie that does not cause Pinocchio's nose to grow. On this occasion, however, he retracts the lie so quickly that it could be argued it does not even count as one.

CHAPTER 33

143. In fact, the narrator does know, because Lampwick reappears briefly, in the final chapter.

144. The word that Collodi uses, *dialetto*, is one that would have
     been on the lips of all Italians at the time as they struggled to un-
     derstand one another in the decades following Unification. Until
     the declaration of the Kingdom of Italy in 1861, standard Italian
     was strictly a minority tongue, used in literature and for com-
     munication among those few citizens of the various states on the
     Italian peninsula who had access to education. One authorita-
     tive estimate, by the linguist Tullio De Mauro, put the propor-
     tion of Italians who could speak standard Italian in 1861 at just
     2.5 percent. Getting them to learn a mutually comprehensible
     language came to be seen as a vital part of nation-building, not
     least by Collodi. And since disseminating Italian depended on
     spreading literacy, education and nation-building became inex-
     tricably linked. Collodi's enthusiasm for education and the em-
     phasis he placed on its importance in the *Adventures* were both
     functions of his patriotism. Subsequently, military service, radio,
     and television also encouraged the use of Italian. But the "dia-
     lects," which linguists regard in some cases as separate lan-
     guages, have proved resilient. According to a survey carried out
     in 2015 by the national statistics office, among Italians above the
     age of six, less than half, 46 percent, spoke only Italian at home.
     Another 32 percent spoke both Italian and in "dialect," while 14
     percent spoke mainly in "dialect." The remainder spoke a for-
     eign language. But perhaps the more surprising conclusion was
     that the use of "dialect" was rising among young adults: it had
     leapt from less than 4 percent in 2000 to more than 12 percent
     in 2015. Source: ISTAT.
145. It can be argued that Italians have been unified as much by food
     as by language. Here is Collodi, a mere thirteen years after the
     completion of Unification, citing two dishes from cities almost
     five hundred miles apart, apparently confident that his readers
     will be familiar with them both.
146. The circus is being staged not under a "big tent" but in a the-
     ater specially converted for the purpose.
147. Girls are otherwise remarkably absent from the *Adventures*,
     with the exception of the Little Girl who turns into a Fairy. But
     then at the time Italian society was highly patriarchal.
148. The original Italian is just as ludicrous and erroneous. With the
     Ringmaster's absurdly pretentious speeches, strewn with the
     most ridiculous mistakes, Collodi is parodying the quasi-
     scientific patter of the charlatans who traveled from town to
     town in nineteenth-century Italy selling bogus merchandise of

all sorts to the impressionable. Their American counterparts were the "snake oil salesmen."

149. Another nod in the direction of contemporary fashion. The camellia had first arrived in Italy from East Asia in the late eighteenth century. But around the middle of the following century the popularity of the flowers was such that it came to be dubbed *cameliomania*. The area between Lucca and Pistoia, which includes the town of Collodi, where the author grew up, was found to be particularly suited to the cultivation of camellias. It is a prime commercial growing area for the flowers to this day.

150. A reference, albeit by means of the wrong adjective, to the work of Franz Joseph Gall (1758–1828), the controversial founder of phrenology, a pseudoscience that purported to be able to define an individual's personality by means of studying the contours of his or her skull.

151. Some of the cures offered by the traveling salesmen that Collodi was satirizing (see note 148) were for hair loss. Hence the reference to the regenerative bulb. As for the "Pyrrhic dance," it appears to be pure nonsense.

152. Another reason not to become a donkey: you will not be able to express yourself or your feelings and will never be taken seriously.

153. See notes 39 and 41.

154. Having a tough hide has a different meaning in Italian from its meaning in English. It signifies that the owner of the hide is resistant to pain and hard work and will not die easily. It figures in the phrase *avere la pelle di ciuco* ("to have the hide of a donkey").

CHAPTER 34

155. Pinocchio is being sarcastic. The point that would have been obvious to Collodi's readers is that Saint Anthony is the saint who protects animals, not humans.

156. The word used by Collodi is *ghiotti* (singular, *ghiotto*). It is symptomatic of the Italians' love of food that they should have three words for "greedy" or "gluttonous," the others being *goloso* and *ingordo*. But just as significantly, only the last signals unequivocal disapproval. The others convey an attitude of relish, of uninhibited sensual appreciation. *Ghiotto,* moreover, can also be used to describe a dish or a kind of food, where it takes on the meaning of "appetizing," "delectable."

157. Attila (d. 453), the ruler of the Hunnish empire who came to be known as "the Scourge of God," is a figure who looms large in the Italians' collective psyche as the personification of wanton destructiveness. He invaded Italy in 452 and laid waste to parts of the north before turning back.

158. Literary history is full of stories of human beings disappearing into whales, notably the biblical prophet Jonah. So why does Collodi opt instead to have Pinocchio swallowed by a shark, a *pescecane*? Italian literary critics have proposed two explanations. One derives from Collodi's having already written, in *Giannettino*, published in 1877, that whales, despite their large mouths, had narrow throats. He knew it was impossible to be swallowed by a whale and he did not want to deny the validity of what he had written in his earlier work. A second theory is that he is again using his fable to hint at an evil in society: in the same way as usurers are described in English as "loan sharks," they were described in late nineteenth-century Florence as *pescecani*—and still are. Collodi's own father had fallen into the clutches of a moneylender: Girolamo Pagliano, who built, among other things, the Teatro Verdi in Florence, which is still an important theater. According to Giuseppe Garbarino in *Pinocchio svelato* (2014), Collodi came to the aid of his father by indebting himself with Pagliano. As in the *Adventures*, father and son both experienced what it was like to end up in the "belly of the shark."

159. A further example of Collodi's habit of adding a dash of humor to lighten the narrative before or after the most frightening passages.

160. In describing the Tuna's voice, Collodi again uses a musical instrument, as he did with the crab in chapter 27. Collodi was a music critic of distinction. He could have used other instruments to illustrate the voices of his sea creatures but chose two that children of his day would have heard on the streets.

161. In other words, ending up in a jar as *tonno sott'olio* (tuna in oil).

CHAPTER 35

162. During Lent, Italians in several parts of the country enjoy a brief, midway celebration, the *mezza quaresima*. The festivities traditionally include the consumption of fried food, including fish.

163. Collodi's account of the shark's devouring of Pinocchio is uncannily similar to a passage that Ariosto wrote for *Orlando furioso* but that he deleted from the final version of his poem. In it, Ruggiero is swallowed by a whale who takes in "a large gulp of water." Once inside, he "sees far away in the cavern a tiny little light from a lamp" and finds an old man, who was also completely white. That could be pure coincidence. But it is worthy of note that the five *canti* deleted from *Orlando furioso* had been published in Florence in 1857 in *Opere minori in verso e in prosa di L. Ariosto*, edited by F. L. Polidori.

164. *Tortellini bolognesi*, pasta rings stuffed with pork, egg, Parmesan cheese, and nutmeg, are usually served in a light broth. So they are normally swallowed with liquid.

165. The point at which Pinocchio goes from being a child to being an adult. He is no longer someone in need of protection, but rather a protector. What follows casts his earlier misadventures in a comparatively positive light, because they have given him the resources and the courage to deal with a perilous situation. Collodi was a strong believer in the value of the "university of life"—of acting according to one's own judgment and learning from one's own mistakes. In a note found among his papers and cited by Maria Jole Minicucci in "Tra fantasia e didattica: Oscillazioni collodiane" in *Pinocchio oggi* (1978), he wrote: "The best practical education that a boy can have is what he learns by himself. . . . It cannot be learned from books." But while Pinocchio is now brave and capable of making important decisions, he still needs to acquire an education in order to become a fully rounded human being.

166. Geppetto was certainly not alone. Even though the vast majority of Italians have always lived close to the sea, until they started going to the seaside as vacationers in the twentieth century, very few knew how to swim. But then large stretches of the Italian coastline were malarial—places to be avoided.

167. Collodi changed this word in his manuscript from *viottola* (a country lane) to *viottolone*, which is the word used to describe a wide carriageway leading to a great house. He may well have had in mind the tree-lined drive that once led to the Villa Reale in Castello. It was called the Viottolone, even in official documents. When visitors to Florence arrive by air, their planes touch down at Amerigo Vespucci airport on a runway that ends just a few hundred yards from where the Viottolone begins. The Viottolone still runs through a park to the Villa

Reale, nowadays the home of the Accademia della Crusca (see pages xxii–xxiii).

168. Collodi is here conferring on Pinocchio the status of a great hero. The son who carries his father to safety is a recurrent theme in literature, most notably in the *Aeneid,* in which Aeneas carries his father, Anchises, to safety from the burning ruins of Troy.

CHAPTER 36

169. The final chapter is unusually long. But then Collodi was in a hurry. While the story was still coming out in the *Giornale per i bambini,* he had signed a contract for the publication of the *Adventures.* The final installment appeared on January 25, 1883, and the manuscript must have been delivered to the publishers almost immediately, because the book itself was already being reviewed on February 11. Ornella Castellani Pollidori, in her critical edition of *Le avventure di Pinocchio* (1983), speculates that the revision may also have fallen victim to what she describes as his "legendary laziness, which always led him, by his own admission, to work the indispensable minimum."

170. See note 166.

171. This is almost certainly untrue. If so, it is at least the fifth instance, and the fourth in the second run of installments, of Pinocchio's lying without his nose growing. But on this occasion the lie is a well-intentioned one, meant to buoy up Geppetto's spirits, and that would seem to be the reason why there are no consequences.

172. The first edition of the *Adventures* in book form, which has been used by most translators since, had *ajutatemi* ("save *me*"). But what Collodi wrote in his manuscript and what was published in the serialization in the *Giornale per i bambini* was *ajutatevi* ("save yourself"), which is more consistent with Pinocchio's rapidly waning egocentricity and his growing sense of responsibility toward Geppetto. Pollidori in her critical edition of the *Adventures* considered *ajutatemi* to be a typographical error. We have accepted her judgment.

173. Since it is unusual for all but small children to give a kiss on the mouth to anyone who is not a lover, some commentators have speculated that it was appropriate in this instance since the Tuna is not a human being. But it could also be a way of show-

ing that, despite his sudden adoption of responsible, adult behavior, Pinocchio remains a "child."

174. Pinocchio and Geppetto are apparently back to where the story
began and will soon meet other characters from the early chapters of the book. Yet until he was swallowed by the shark, Pinocchio had not left the island to which he had swum from a
beach that was six hundred miles away. Nor could the shark
have covered the distance in the very short time that Pinocchio
was in its belly.

175. The idiosyncratic, original phrasing is *"Addio mascherine!,"*
which literally means "Farewell, little masks," the masks repre-
senting trickery. *"Mascherine"* is used here and in some other
expressions to let another person know that you have understood their game.

176. Though this phrase appears several times in the narrative, its
use here at the very end of the book creates a striking parallel
with the beginning. Pinocchio begins his adventures as a piece
of firewood "like all the others" and ends it as a boy "like all
the others."

177. Remember who was last wearing ankle boots? The donkeys pulling the Little Man's coach who had once been boys. It is a chill-
ing reminder of the fate that Pinocchio so narrowly avoided.

178. This the only time in the entire book that Collodi uses the tech-
nically correct term to describe Pinocchio. See note 13.

179. Few punctuation marks have unleashed the expenditure of
more ink than the ellipsis points at the very end of the *Adventures.* Italian commentators have been speculating ever since on
what Collodi intended. Was he creating the freedom he might
need for a sequel? Was he intimating that perhaps Pinocchio
would not stay good forever? Or was he staking a claim to that
ambiguity of meaning that underlies so many great creative
works? What did the author himself have to say about his ending? An acquaintance, Ermenegildo Pistelli, a priest and phi-
lologist, claimed in *Eroi, uomini e ragazzi* (1926) that Collodi
was once asked the question. Pistelli quoted him as replying: "I
don't remember having ended it like that."